Thorns of Roses

A NOVEL

Copyright ©2020 by Sheba Rasheed

All Rights Reserved. Except as permitted under the U.S. Copyright Act of 1976 no part of this publication may be reproduced, distributed or transmitted in any form or by any means, or stored in a database or retrieval system, without the prior written permission of the publisher.

ISBN 9781736257210

Sheba Rasheed Publishing, LLC Written by Sheba A. Rasheed.

Cover Design by Octavious Hose–Clever Motifs LLC Cover Photo by Glenn Miller Photography

Thorns of Roses

A NOVEL

By Sheba Rasheed

Acknowledgements

I am humbled that my Creator thought me worthy of this process and promise.

"Thank You" is not enough to express the tremendous gratitude and love I have for my parents, Prentice and Shukriyyah. For the blessings and lessons that we faced as a family, it was faith, love, and forgiveness that always held us together.

Mother, there are no words for the intangible gifts you have bestowed upon your children. You are the epitome of the woman I aspire to be.

Childhood memories of visiting South Georgia, spending time with my maternal and paternal grandparents still bring smiles to my face. Horseback riding, helping my Grandma Josie "shell peas" on the porch, and swinging my legs from my Grandma Equilla's yard swing… all woven fibers into the fabric of my life.

Family and Friends, thank you for sharing your love and light with me.

Dedications

I could not have known that a chance encounter with you, ***Louis,*** would help to shape the woman I would become. This story would not be possible without the memories that I treasure. Your first gift to me was your friendship. The second was your love. The final and most precious gift is our daughter. I am forever grateful for the time and space that we were allowed to share **on earth and beyond.**

Taahira,

The biggest smile I've ever seen on your father's face occurred the day you were born. There are some things that happen in life that are unexplainable, irreversible, and change our lives forever. If I could give you anything, it would be more time to bask in his love. I pray you will always feel how loved you are in heaven and on earth and share the power of that love with the world.

Prologue

To Be Absent from the Body is to be Present with the Lord 2 Corinthians 5:8

How could the sun be shining so brightly on the worst day of my life? Despite the beaming golden sunrays and warm climate, my world was dark and cold. As I sat grief-stricken surrounded by family and friends under the green tent, my eyes flooded with tears staring blankly upon the shiny black casket adorned with polished chrome and beautiful blooming yellow roses. The windows to my soul, had transformed into a deep well from which a steady stream of warm tears were drawn unto my face. I couldn't breathe; suffocating in the blackest pit of darkness I'd never experienced before. Surrounded by people that came to pay their respect, offer condolences, be nosy, or the haters that came to witness first hand the inconsolable grief of others.

Chapter One

Nia's childhood could best be described as a rose garden; beautiful from afar but the closer you got, the more likely you were to see and feel the pain of the inescapable thorns.

Her hand-on-hip, take-no-mess, keep 'em at arms length personality was shaped by the loving yet tumultuous childhood she shared with her mother, father, and younger sister. It was a budding life of ups and downs during great family times spent together and not-so great times spent torn in the middle of two divided parents. Nia enjoyed the best of both worlds, adventurous, fun-filled summers in the country, enjoying life between her maternal and paternal grandparents' farms in the southern region of Georgia and the majestic ambiance of growing up in Miami, where people from all over the world traveled by air, rail or boat to experience the tropical paradise of never ending beaches, blazing sunshine, streets lined with tall, towering palm trees, and intoxicating nightlife.

Despite the good intentions of both her parents to give their daughters a life of opportunity and promise, relational challenges continuously threatened the family's cohesiveness. As with most divorces, there is usually more than one good reason for the decision to split and by age 7 Nia had lived with many stark contradictions of love and indifference, security and vulnerability, love and heartbreak. If it was true that diamonds were formed under pressure, young Nia had no idea that her life would include the precise amount of pressure and timing to become VVS 1 diamond certified.

Her baby sister, Jasmine, was five years younger than Nia and seemingly unable to fully comprehend this potentially life altering trauma to a child's psyche. To witness acts of extreme violence against their mother by the man who had stood before God, not once but twice vowing to love and protect her was enough to cause irreparable damage to a young girl's perception of herself and her father, the person she was supposed to be able to trust as her protector in the world in which she lives.

Nia's father was a complex man born into a complicated historical time period, growing up in the segregated rural south, he was aware yet defenseless against the human degradation that befell nearly anyone of color. Being born into the grips of injustice, oppression, and dehumanization of blacks in the color-divided United States of America set the course for internal conflict and external war. However, the scales of balance tilted in his favor as he was born to a master masonry and the privileged daughter of a southern entrepreneurial legend while his friends' parents were mostly sharecropping. Even still, formal schooling for a strong, young, black boy wasn't a priority and at the age of 18, he enlisted in the US Army and later served in the Vietnam War.

Time would prove that like most soldiers, he left one way and returned another. How does one leave a war that won't leave him?

Upon his return to the United States, as he adjusted to life after the military, he met, courted and married Nia's mom, Belle, also from a small rural southern town in Georgia about an hour south of Macon. Belle graduated with honors from the racially segregated high school in Hawkinsville, GA. Periodically, she would share stories with her daughters of how even though the books were tattered, the teachers were tough and failure was never an option. Belle's mother, the matriarch of her family, affectionately known as Mun, encouraged her daughter to relocate to South Florida to pursue better opportunities than were available at home. With the support of both parents, Belle remembered her dad telling her right before she got on the Greyhound bus, "Never forget, no matter what happens, you can always come home".

It was during her pursuit of a Bachelor of Arts Degree at Florida International University, in Miami, Florida, that she encountered Pop. Though both had been taught the importance of strong work ethic, education, family, and faith, the woes of unresolved pressure would prove ineffable. Pop learned the important lessons of strategic thinking in a kill or be killed war and world. He'd survived a childhood rooted in the inequality of the south and a historic war. Upon his return to the states, he mastered the skills of a fine jeweler and became the go-to for locals and many black celebrities from all over the country.

As a father, he took pride in showering his daughters with the fancies that made little girls smile like visits to the pristine beaches of Miami, the downtown Miami Omni Mall's merry-go round, out-of- state family vacations and of course the dancing diamond baubles that even young girls' eyes lit up for. But just like every coin has a head and a tail, when angered, he didn't hesitate to show his tail. He had a dark side that would leave his wife and daughters in fright or flight mode on many occasions.

After years of physical and emotional abuse hurled upon Belle by Pop, as her daughters stood by defenseless, Belle made a courageous and maybe even life-saving decision to walk away from a nine-year marriage that she had paid for literally with blood, sweat, and tears.

The split of Nia's family was a somber new beginning for her mother, who was a schoolteacher, and her two girls. Pop adamantly fought against the divorce but after recuperating from a surgical procedure that required more than seventeen stitches, Belle knew that this was not the example or life she wanted for their children. Not to mention, she hated to think of how Pop's anger could one-day escalate to an irreversible outcome that could leave their daughters without one or both parents.

Like the aftermath of a severe South Florida hurricane, the storm would calm, and the sun would arise again. The damage had been done and rebuilding was a tough process for the newly single mom. Belle was raised in a two-parent, loving home and couldn't imagine the separation of her family but she held her head up high, watching the City of North Miami Police officers escort Pop out of the front door with slight but non-violent resistance. Nia and Jasmine somberly stood at the screened bar door watching daddy leave as their mother stood a few feet behind them with tears in the corner of her eyes. Belle had no idea where the road ahead may lead but she was sure she couldn't continue down the path she'd been on.

Family traditions continued like soul food Sunday dinner with family and friends stopping by for a full plate or maybe just some peach cobbler with vanilla ice cream atop; African dance class on Saturday mornings at the Joseph Caleb Center which was a haven for the youth of Liberty City, one my Miami's notorious areas where little girls grew up too fast and boys found their manhood in the challenges of the streets, Girls Scouts on Saturday afternoons, praise and worship on Sundays. Monday thru Fridays, mama worked as a full-time teacher in the day and part-time teacher at the Juvenile Justice Center at night to supplement the additional family income that left when Pop left.

The devastation of her divided family taught Nia some life lessons that she vowed to remember for the future of her own adult life: never ever let a man put his hands on you to hurt you, protect what you love at all costs, work to win, and hold your chin up especially when it would be easier to bow your head in tears. Nia and Jasmine quickly adjusted to a peaceful and nurturing home life. As the years progressed, being the daughters of an educator proved rewarding and annoying simultaneously. There was always someone at home to help with the homework assignments and projects but there was no room for mediocrity. Being held to a high standard was the expectation and anything short of excellence was frowned upon.

After the divorce was finalized, sole custody of the girls were awarded to Ms. Ali and visiting rights to Pop. Initially, this seemed to be cool with everyone involved but it wasn't long before the coin flipped to tail and Pop began showing out. In the beginning, he would arrive and knock on the door, receive Nia and Jasmine and off they would go for a day of fun, dining, shopping, or anything their hearts desired. Each one couldn't wait to return home to show Mama what new gift they'd gotten that day. But it wasn't before long when Pop would arrive and try to force Mama into conversations of reconciliation, "Baby, I miss my family. You know scripture says that man is not meant to live alone and I don't want anyone else raising my daughters". Each week there was a new scripture and stronger conviction on his behalf to earn his family back. Fortunately, it never turned physical and Pop genuinely appeared to want to redeem himself and restore his family. He began to realize that Ms. Ali was resolute in her decision to not subject herself or her children to the chaos they'd managed to survive and escape, the rejection took its toll and he became more distant.

Chapter Two

The Luke Skywalker Concert was the talk of Miami; especially in the local high schools that Nia and her friends attended. The girls had spent most of their week half listening to the drones of their teachers as they planned to be fully entertained by antics that only Uncle Luke and his crew could pull off. The Saturday of the concert was spent in the most popular nail and hair salon in North Dade. The hair stylists, nail techs, clients, and solicitors were all entertainers within their own right. People came to see and be seen, wearing fly gear and fresh kicks, telling stories of the trifling men in their lives and the great extent they were willing to go to keep them. It was definitely pre-show entertainment for the girls.

As Nia prepared for the evening, she smiled at the thought of her small circle of friends because each person brought something unique to the clique and she loved their chemistry. Nia was the eldest of two daughters. She was the insightful, studious, and quick witted one. Sasha was the extrovert whose friendly demeanor got the girls lots of perks such as the complimentary tickets to the concert; her family knew everyone who was in anyone in Miami and she tended to be the life of the party. Mya, was an only child of a single mother who worked as a private nurse for some of South Florida's wealthiest elderly, was known for her model-like height and exotic features that made most guys do double takes. But make no mistake; she was feisty and fearless; wiling to kick off her shoes on the spin of a dime if someone violated her personal space without an invitation.

Fresh out of the shower, Nia caught the last couple of questions of television news journalist, Felicia Devoe and Miami Mayor Velasquez as clips of explicit video and hip hop lyrics flashed across the screen.

"Mayor, do you think the lyrics of Luke Skywalker are appropriate for the age demographics that are likely to attend this evening's concert"?

"Well, Felicia, these are not the lyrics or images that I would promote for the youth and young adults in our communities, however, parents have to take responsibility in the activities their children are exposed to".

Channel 9 WTVR's Felicia Devoe, closed her interview with her final question, "Will you be attending Mr. Mayor?", only to receive a quick and bold, "NO" in response as he was whisked away by an entourage of staff prepping him for his fifth media appointment today.

As Sasha pulled her mom's new white BMW 525 into the parking lot of the Miami Baseball Stadium, she checked her nude colored tinted lip gloss, used her old school pink sponge for the oil on her face, and brushed her signature shoulder length wrapped hair down. She exited the car and strolled to the admissions gate to meet her friends as they'd discussed. Mya and Sasha had known each other since elementary school but Nia had met them both during middle school. Nia was the first to notice Sasha dressed in all white wearing clear rhinestone framed fashion glasses first and waved her hand so that she could see them. Mya was dressed in light denim jeans with the shredded slits down the front of each pant leg complimented by a fluorescent yellow shirt with the distressed, ripped back and grey stiletto heels with silver spikes on the toe; Nia kept it cool but classy as usual, opting for an all black denim jean and jacket set with a graffiti inspired paint graphic on the back of the jacket. Nia wasn't shy but her mama had been telling her since she could remember that God gave us two ears and one mouth so that we should listen more than we speak. Hence, the reason she chose to play the background and observe whatever was going on around her. As Sasha reached her friends, she was full of anticipation for a great night of fun with her girls. Luke was sure to not disappoint and the show was predicted to be one of the hottest and most talked about performances of 1989. As the girls entered the admissions gate, they were intoxicated with the high energy of the other attendees and the sky was illuminated by bright stars; tonight was sure to be entertaining, full of fun, and memorable.

It seemed like Nia had just laid down for bed but the bright sun shining through the window's blinds reminded her that last night was everything she thought it would be and though she was sure her parents' wouldn't have approved, Uncle Luke and the Two Live Crew did not disappoint the field of fans that had attended. Still half sleep, Nia reached for the ringing phone. No sooner than she could say "hello", Sasha began babbling about a guy that had given his cousin, Junior, a friend of Sasha's, his phone number from the night before for Nia to call him.

After a night of partying, hanging out with friends, and enjoying the show, Nia just couldn't understand where all of Sasha's energy was coming from. They all were too young to drink and too afraid of their parents to experiment with recreational drugs but the night of music, dancing, and fun had truly proven to create a natural high for all. After finally getting Sasha to give her a full head to toe description of the guy, Nia proceeded with the girlfriend grill and drill.

"Where does he attend school? What neighborhood is he from? What's his dress code? What's his reputation? Who has he dated? Why does he want *me to call him*? Why didn't he just give me his phone number himself?"

Sasha had to squeal a loud "Listen girl, either you can call him or don't but he's a real laid back guy, he's always wearing the latest kicks, and he's the only junior in high school that I know driving to school in a tricked out truck."

That was enough for Nia to know that anything more she wanted to know about "Jihad", she was going to have to get directly from the source himself and she had no problem with that. "Give him my number; if he wants to talk, now's his chance," Nia told Sasha. The girls chatted a little more about who wore what, who was with whom, and how the standing room only concert was all they had expected it to be with dancers whose movement antics showed how they were as fluid as water. After a full discussion of the concert's highlights, the girls ended their laughter and agreed to talk at school tomorrow.

Chapter Three

The summer was rapidly approaching and Nia and her friends were eagerly anticipating the endless possibilities of sunny South Florida, Miami to be exact. There was nothing like the summer jams hosted by the best DJs from the various neighborhoods of South Dade all the way to the county line road that separated North Dade from Broward County, hosted on the beautiful beaches of Crandon, Haulover, Ft. Lauderdale, and the famous South Beach. This was going to be the last summer before Nia and her friends' senior year of high school and they planned to party, shop, and prepare for one of the biggest milestones of their lives.

As Nia and Jasmine chilled in the bedroom that they shared, the telephone could be heard ringing in the living room.

"Nia, come get the phone", mama yelled. Nia rushed to the phone, thinking it was one of her girlfriend's calling with plans to add some excitement to the afternoon; however, when she said, "hello", it was an unfamiliar male voice on the other end of the line.

"Hello, Nia?" the guy replied. "Yes, who is this", Nia asked.

"This is Jihad, Junior's cousin. I got your number from Sasha".

Nia thought to herself, "he sounds so confident" so she figured she'd put him on the spot and see how he responded. "Yeah, Sasha *tried to give me your number* but why didn't you give it to me yourself'? The phone line was silent for a few seconds and then Jihad replied, "I kept watching you but you don't look like someone that would be single and since I didn't know your status, I chose to put the ball in your court to avoid any conflict. But since we're on the phone, I don't have to worry about that."

Now it was Nia's turn to leave the phone line silent for a few seconds. Jihad had not only complimented her but also demonstrated a degree of maturity that most guys her age didn't possess. It was just the introduction but she was thinking she already kind of liked him. Jihad asked Nia did she want to go to the movies and then Bayside, a casual waterfront outdoor shopping and dining area in the heart of downtown Miami? She was happy he had asked and agreed to be ready by 3:00 p.m. Nia immediately called Sasha and gave her the full details of her first conversation with Jihad, their movie plans, and her first thoughts of him. Sasha rolled her eyes towards the ceiling as if Nia could see her because she had tried to tell this girl that Jihad was far from average but Nia being Nia went into a full personality analysis mode before she had ever spoken with Jihad for herself.

As Nia searched her closet for something that would be cute but comfortable considering the scorching heat outside and the cool temperature of the movie theatre, she decided upon a cute multi-color romper, metallic sandals that complimented her pedicured toes, denim jacket for inside the theater, and a stylish leather clutch to compliment her outfit. The closer it got to 3:00, she felt butterflies in her stomach; why? She couldn't quite put her finger on it but there was something about Jihad and she would soon find out what it was.

The doorbell rang and Nia's mom welcomed Jihad inside. Jihad was dressed in a royal blue Sean John graphic t-shirt, dark denim jeans, and matching suede and leather Bally sneakers. Nia liked his style; not flashy but fashionable. As Ms. Ali gave Jihad a full look over, she had a warm smile but a cold mental list of questions that would rival the best criminal TV show's best interrogation. If Jihad had impressed Nia during their first conversation, impressing Ms. Ali would not prove as easy. Being a woman, a divorcee, mother of two growing daughters and an educator of middle and high school students for many years, Ms. Ali had seen the trappings of relationships of all ages and backgrounds and just wanted to make sure Jihad and Nia gave themselves time to get to know each other without peer pressure or rushed expectations. She had no intention of sitting idly by as her college-bound daughter began to learn how to navigate the maze of dating.

Jihad seemed reserved and remained cool as Ms. Ali went through her list of expectations and requirements in exchange for her permission to accompany her daughter to the movies. Jihad pretty much let Ms. Ali do all the talking, responding only when asked a direct question as Nia sat by silently praying for this necessary preliminary test to end. Ms. Ali ended her "mama speech" with a hug for Nia and a firm handshake that said, "I'm not playing with you boy!" for Jihad.

As the twosome exited the beautifully landscaped yard, Jihad hit the alarm to unlock the door and as if on queue, opened Nia car door as Ms. Ali watched from her bedroom window. One of the hottest radio stations of South Florida, 99.1 JAMZ was playing and neither Nia nor Jihad said much during the fifteen-minute ride from Nia's house to Bayside. They both seemed to be feeling hesitant yet filled with anticipation about what lie ahead for as they sat back and enjoyed the vibe of the music that was playing.

When they arrived, Jihad walked around and opened Nia's door as she thought to herself, "he seems really nice" but Nia wasn't quick to let her guards down. The lessons she learned from her dad of head and tail lay dormant in the back of her mind. During the movie, it surprised Nia that Jihad had not made one attempt to hold her hand or put his arm around the back of her seat. He had purchased all the snacks she wanted, nachos with cheese and extra jalapeno peppers, medium popcorn with light butter, medium Coca-Cola, and cherry Twizzlers. He gave her the preference of where she'd like to sit but besides that he didn't make any typical moves that she and her girlfriends had discussed about other guys.

After exiting the action-thriller movie, Nia and Jihad thought about what they would eat. Bayside had dining for every budget or preference including the food court, Hooters, and specialty restaurants. Nia thought she and Jihad would probably eat in the food court like she and her friends usually did but he suggested Pier 66. During their stroll towards the restaurant, they both chatted about the movies highlights until they reached Pier 66, a waterfront seafood restaurant that served the best broiled-lobster tails, sautéed shrimp, scallops, and crab and seafood rice, and lightly garlic butter steamed asparagus tips in the downtown area. As they waited for the check,

Nia and Jihad talked about the schools they attended, family life, and hobbies and interests. As the waiter sat the small black leather folder that had the check enclosed, Jihad reached in his pocket and pulled out a large wad of cash that he held beneath the table as he peeled off the tab and tip and put the rest of the money back in his pocket. "You ready?" he asked. Nia rose from her seat and they headed towards the shopping area.

Jihad may not have known it but Nia was definitely checking out his demeanor; so far he had gotten pass Ms. Ali's security questions, behaved like a gentleman, and was becoming more intriguing to Nia by the second. It was clear that he hadn't paid for lunch with a weekly allowance like the one Nia and her younger sister received, she thought to herself, "what was really up with him?" As Jihad followed NIa in and out of all the hottest boutiques, she noticed how he didn't complain or rush her like her older male cousins' girlfriends had grumbled about the way they behaved in the mall. As they walked towards the frozen smoothie kiosk, Jihad ordered a mango-colada smoothie and asked if Nia would like one? She ordered strawberry- banana and he asked if she wanted to take a ride on the Fun Cruise that sailed every hour along the Miami intercostal where the majestic Miami skyline and celebrity homes could be seen from a distance. Even though Nia wasn't ready to end the date with Jihad, she knew not to push Mama's buttons and decided another time would be best. He was like Sasha said, laid back and of very few words. NIa could tell he was checking her out too, from head to toe. Nia had experienced a couple of mutual high school crushes in the past but she never had an official boyfriend. Some of the girls she knew had not only had boyfriends but a few even had a baby. Jihad seemed cool but only time would tell if their new friendship would fizzle or sizzle during the summer months to come.

Chapter Four

*S*ummer came and went so fast it made Nia's head spin. She and her girls had definitely had a pre-senior year summer to remember! The beach parties, shopping for the latest gear at some of the best indoor and outdoor shopping boutiques, malls, and fashion districts that Miami life offered. Besides, the hoopla of summer fun, Nia received several letters from colleges she had applied to and when she saw the beige envelope with green and orange embossed lettering in the return address, she almost hit the roof as she yelled and screamed in excitement. She hadn't even opened it yet but she just knew; it had to be the moment she had anticipated over the years of attending middle school, high school, college tours, and the Upward Bound Program. This had to be THE moment where her preparation and opportunity would meet and set the course of her dreams of success. She held the ivory linen envelope with the bright orange and bold green embossed letters trimmed in metallic gold so tightly as she contemplated opening it alone or sharing the moment with her sister and mom. To be actually holding her decision letter from the internationally acclaimed historically black university, Florida Agricultural & Mechanical University was enough to send her to cloud nine. To add icing to the cake,

Nia and Jihad had gone out several more times and Nia was beginning to like him a lot.

She had learned that his family owned a few dry cleaning businesses and that Jihad worked at the location closest to her home. Jihad actually lived in North Dade in a palatial residence that seemed like a mansion compared to the modest middle class home Nia shared with her mom and sister. Jihad lived with his mom, step-dad, and two older sisters. All three siblings attended their neighborhood high school, which was on the opposite end of the South Dade schools that Nia and her sister attended.

Jihad was an enigma to Nia in many ways. At seventeen, he didn't appear to socialize with but a few people outside his immediate family circle; he wasn't exactly shy but he didn't speak without having anything meaningful to say, he was a good listener and his smile started in his eyes; but more than anything, he was focused on getting money. Nia had just as many guy friends as girlfriends but had never encountered anyone in her age group who'd rather focus on his money grind than hanging out with his neighborhood homeboys.

Nia and Jihad had both returned to their respective schools in the fall or so she thought. Jihad would call Nia and invite her to one of their favorite Latin restaurants, Laguna's, and as badly as she wanted to put her homework to the side and ride out with Jihad, she knew that she had to pull a strong grade point average to stay eligible for the scholarship money she'd applied for to attend college. What she came to like and eventually love about Jihad was that he would still go to the

THORNS OF ROSES

restaurant alone, order three entrees and return to Nia's house for a brief homework break that she and Jasmine enjoyed while their mom worked her part-time teaching job at the Juvenile Justice Detention Center.

Ms. Ali's very observant and protective nature led to her affinity for Jihad. She really appreciated him taking time to check not only on Nia but also Jasmine as she continued to work three evenings a week on her part-time job. She had seen many young men over the years **within the Miami-Dade County Public School System** and had become pretty good at distinguishing the good and bad apples. Despite how she approved of Nia's and Jihad's budding friendship, she still had one concern about Jihad; he didn't seem interested in school life. She had asked him in the past about his favorite subjects or future plans after high school but besides a brief mentioning of liking math, he didn't talk much about school.

Nia then became the focus of Ms. Ali's inquisition about Jihad's future plans. Nia was beginning to despise the constant questioning. Jihad was nice, attentive, cool to be around, and protective of Nia, Jasmine, and his own two sisters. Nia didn't want Ms. Ali to run Jihad away with all the "teacher talk". As senior year activities' began to take place like Pep Rallies, Senior Skip Day, Superlative Seniors' Voting, Grad Nite, and other memorable once-in-a-lifetime events, Jihad never seemed to mention the activities taking place at his own school. Although Nia and Jihad hung out together as typical teenager couples do; movie dates, family gatherings, school sporting events and more, neither had spoken of an official relationship. It was just like the quote Nia's uncles' had said many times before, "What's understood doesn't need to be explained". Neither had felt the need to ask or confirm his or her growing feelings for one another; it was evident to anyone that could see.

Chapter Five

It was to be the Sweet 16 birthday bash of all sweet 16 extravaganzas. Nia's guest list included family and friends that spanned from South Dade to Palm Beach County. She had a large number of cousins from both her maternal and paternal sides not to mention classmates since elementary school.

Nia's mom had only allowed her to attend the neighborhood schools during the summer breaks of middle and high school. During the regular school year, she attended schools in the Coral Gables area, an affluent and predominately white demographic. Most of the black students that attended the high school were bused in from Coconut Grove, a historically predominately black community with roots that traveled from the sunny skies of South Florida to the beautiful Caribbean islands of Bahamas.

So Nia's circle of friends and friends of friends had grown over the years and she was looking forward to celebrating her 16th birthday with the people she'd grown up with in just a couple of weeks. Ms. Ali had always worked hard to give her daughters the life that had escaped her growing up in the rural south. Not that she had any regrets, she had always had what she needed but she was happy to give her daughters some of the things she used to dream of growing up.

It was Saturday morning and Nia had solicited the help of her girlfriends to pick out a dress for the party. As Nia headed south on NW 22nd avenue, towards the upscale shoppes of Miracle Mile where beautiful palm trees lined the sides of the streets. The dining cuisine reflected the various cultures and people that called Miami home. Cuban, Benihana, Chinese buffets, Ruth Chris Steakhouse, Italian eateries, and more made the visit to this fashion enclave even more special. Miracle Mile was notably famous for hosting all the best to offer in the industry of weddings and prom boutiques.

As Nia continued towards their destination, the girls chit-chatted and caught up on what had been going on in their lives at home, school, and in the unofficial neighborhood news. Since Maliki and Sasha attended the same neighborhood high school and Nia attended the magnet school where her mom taught, there were always gaps in updates and much needed time to bring each other up to speed.

Sasha was excited about her new friend guy, Pepper, whose nickname was given to him since his childhood days of Pop Warner Football. He was known for being too hot to handle or hold on the recreational fields where the dreams of little boys and their parents began to take flight. Many well-known NFL Players who had been born and raised in Miami had also graced these neighborhood parks and with hard work, skill, sacrifice, and determination, had lived to see their dreams come true. Sasha shared with the girls how she was thinking of giving Pepper *the business* if he played his cards right. He was a star running back on the varsity football team and everyone was talking about how he was destined for a full college athletic scholarship at one of the top Division 1A schools. Both Nia and Mya knew that Sasha loved athletes, especially those that had promising futures. As they listened intently to their friend, they silently and simultaneously hoped that she also played her cards right. Because if she didn't, she wouldn't be the first girl to figure out all too late that a love interest was not only playing football; he was playing her too.

Nia's excitement couldn't be hidden no matter how hard she tried to focus on her girls' updates of life, school, and dating. She was bursting with anticipation, especially since Jihad had briefly mentioned a surprise he had for her big day. She was counting down until her big day and he had only added fuel to her fire by mentioning a "surprise". Nia knew that with Jihad's already reserved demeanor he could and would keep the surprise a secret so she didn't even bother trying to pry the details out of him. Her friends knew that she was getting more and more into him because they had never seen or heard her talk about anyone so much or so seriously.

As Nia pulled into the parking garage, retrieved the parking ticket, and found a parking spot close to the elevator, the girls checked their hair and lip-gloss and proceeded to exit the car. It was a busy Saturday afternoon in the shopping area and the streets were already lined with other small groups of girls and women friends who were on similar quests as Nia.

As the girls strolled down the sidewalk, talking and peering into the various boutique windows, their eyes opened wide with amazement at the beautifully embellished gowns. Some of them appeared to have been designed right in the middle of someone's dream with crystals, pearls, exotic lace, and the tiniest iridescent beads that shimmered through the streak less glass.

Mya asked Nia, "What are we looking for? Long or short, straight or a ball gown, color?"

"Yeah," added Sasha, "We're gonna need some information if we are here to help find "the dress".

Nia thought about it and they were right, she was dress shopping but hadn't really thought about what kind of dress she was looking for.

"All I know is it has to be B-A-D", replied Nia.

As the girls walked in and out of shops perusing the designs and sharing their thoughts, Nia's mind drifted to Jihad. She wondered what he was doing right now and kind of wished she asked him to come instead. Not because he'd be any help; dress shopping was probably the last thing he wanted to be doing but she just enjoyed his presence.

"Nia!" Sasha's voice called Nia back to the task at hand, "What do you think about this one?" Sasha was holding a gorgeous off-white, off-the shoulder long-sleeved dress with the covered torso hand- stitched with crystals that reflected pink, turquoise blue, and light yellow colors depending on how it was held under the boutique's gleaming chandelier.

The bottom of the dress was a beautiful shimmering sateen fabric with a bubble-design. Nia looked up and down the dress in awe. She knew they hadn't been in all of the shops on Miracle Mile but she had seen enough. She was in love with this dress! The sales lady helped Nia get fitted for the alterations, select the accessories that were sure to set the dress off, and check-out with her receipt and pick-up ticket. Nia thought to herself, December was going to be a birthday month to remember.

Chapter Six

There are some days in a girl's life that can only be described as magical and turning sixteen was one of them. Nia's mom had reserved a beautiful banquet hall in Hialeah, which was known as home for some of the most artistic and talented event planners in South Florida. Some of the most creative and talented floral, cake, and decoration designers had shops in the area and were well- respected business people. If you wanted to turn fantasy into reality, this was certainly the place to begin.

Ms. Ali and Nia's aunt, Peaches, had seen and approved the layout earlier. Nia had spent the morning and afternoon being pampered in true diva style, French manicured hands and pedicured toes, hairstyling and lastly the perfect make-up application.

Nia's home telephone was ringing off the hook all day with inquiries about the party venue, dress code, and RSVP confirmations. This was the typical **reaction** of the people who had not only received a personal invitation but had been calling ever since it arrived in the mail! Nia was trying to keep her cool so instead of responding with annoyance, she just decided to unplug the phone for a while to get some peace. "Sorry to anyone with a legitimate question about tonight but I refuse to entertain anyone else who was too lazy to read the invitation," Nia thought to herself.

Time was moving swiftly and the festivities were soon to begin. Nia's dad had offered to pay for a limousine to take her to the party but she had also been asked by Jihad if she'd like him to pick her up. So it was no surprise to anyone when Nia decided to let the limo take mama, Jasmine, Mya, and Sasha, and a few of her close cousins. The tempo was up, and everyone was looking forward to the birthday bash. The only involvement Nia had taken in the planning was the writing the guest list and selecting her own dress, other than that Ms. Ali, her sister, Peaches, and the banquet hall's party coordinator, Ms. Suarez, had taken care of every detail from décor to dinner.

Nia didn't know what to expect but the butterflies in her stomach were an indication of her nervousness. This was the big day she'd been waiting for but the closer it got, it was also a reminder to her of how close graduation was and that meant the time was approaching when she would have to leave Jihad in Miami as she began college life in Tallahassee, FL, at FAMU.

"Nia", Ms. Ali called and snapped Nia back into the moment. "This party will start on time, so I suggest you start getting dressed". "Mama is right, Nia thought. I want to make a grand entrance, but I don't want to miss my own party".

As Ms. Ali began to lay out Nia's attire and accessories for the evening, tears began to well up in her eyes. Her first born was sixteen years old and growing up too fast for any mom's comfort but Ms. Ali was proud and grateful to God that Nia hadn't given her any major problems over the years. Nia's second cousin, Brandon, was a professional photographer and was on hand to capture the magical moments of the evening, beginning with Ms. Ali helping Nia get dressed. Brandon was doing a great job of giving off a paparazzi vibe even as a solo photographer. Nia and her mom looked at their reflections in the mirror, hugged, and prepared to leave. The limo driver had arrived about 20 minutes ago and was patiently sitting in front of the house. Jihad had called and said he was about 15 minutes away due to a fender bender that had been moved to the side on I-95 southbound. So, Ms. Ali gathered everyone together for a touching prayer of gratitude, blessings, and joy. As everyone except for Nia exited the house, the limo driver hopped out of the car and walked to the passenger side to assist them into the luxury stretch vehicle. Random comments of the plush interior and stocked bar of snacks, soft drinks, and champagne were muttered as everyone sat back and enjoyed the ride. The driver played the hottest party music from New Edition to Salt-N-Pepa.

Shortly after everyone left the house, the doorbell rang. NIa, still in her leopard print fuzzy slippers, walked to the door and opened it. Before she could even open the clear security door, a wide smile crossed her face as she saw Jihad dressed in black casual dress pants and a cream and black Versace long sleeve button down shirt on the other side holding a beautiful arrangement of roses. The arrangement was so wide it nearly covered Jihad's face. Jihad playfully rang the doorbell again to remind her that he was *still* outside. Nia opened the door and accepted the floral arrangement from Jihad, retreated to the kitchen to find a vase, and returned to give Jihad the biggest, tightest hug she had ever given him. Jihad told Nia that he had been pre-warned by Ms. Ali to not be delayed in delivering NIa to the hall and he was not taking the friendly but serious reminder lightly. Nia returned to her bedroom to retrieve her shoes and was ready to enjoy her special night.

As they exited the house, Jihad waited for Nia to lock both doors and then gestured for her to walk in front of him towards the car. When Nia turned around towards the car, to her surprise it wasn't Jihad's black truck. Jihad had managed to surprise Nia again; he was escorting her to her birthday party in a silver two-door Porsche sports car that she had never seen him drive before. The night was getting better by the second and she almost wanted to pinch herself to make sure everything was real. She asked Jihad were the flowers and transportation the surprise he'd mentioned and to her delight and excitement, he replied, "Nope". Jihad turned the music up, leaned back, and headed in the direction of the banquet hall. Nia just sat back and silently Thanked God for this indescribable feeling that she never wanted to forget.

Chapter Seven

*I*t was not unusual for Jihad to ride in silence as he leaned back and vibed to his customized music system or listened to Nia bounce from one topic to another but as they pulled into the parking lot, Nia noticed that they had both been unusually silent during the ride to the party. Nia was elated and she hadn't walked inside yet. Jihad parked in one of the Reserved Parking Spots for the guest(s) of honor. One of the banquet hall's attendants opened Jihad's door and Jihad walked around and opened Nia's door. Jihad tipped the uniformed man and the couple headed towards the elevator that led to the penthouse level venue.

As they approached the door, Nia could hear that someone had turned the music down as Auntie Peaches' voice was heard announcing the young lady of the hour, Nia Ali and her boyfriend, Jihad Johnson. Excitement and applause could be heard as Nia and Jihad entered. Jihad, not one for fanfare or the spotlight drifted away from the growing crowd that was surrounding Nia with hugs, birthday wishes, and comments about how beautiful everything was. Nia hadn't even had a chance to take in the decorations because she had been bombarded as soon as she walked in. Auntie Peaches allowed a few more minutes of the festive well wishes and then she brought everyone's attention back to the podium with the sarcastic humor that only Auntie Peaches could.

"Uuuhmm, excuse me, everyone, if you all will please return to your dinner tables, we can get this evening's formalities out of the way, so that we can get this party started before my niece turns sassy seventeen".

Family and friends in attendance laughed at her "I'm joking but also serious" comment and began to settle down.

Ms. Ali approached the podium and retrieved the microphone from its stand as Mr. Ali stood nearby. She walked over to her daughter who was now seated and motioned for her to stand up as she reached for her daughter's hand.

"Today is only one of the many days that a mother looks forward to in a daughter's life. Nia you, my first born, have given me so much joy since the moment your dad and I laid eyes on you. From your first coos to your first grade school photograph with the missing teeth, you have continued to grow into a beautiful young lady. Words alone cannot express how full of love and joy my heart is because you are my daughter. I pray that God continues to bless and protect you as you continue to pursue your dreams. On behalf of your family, we love you, we love you, I love you."

Ms. Ali kissed her daughter, then returned to the front of the room full of loved ones and thanked everyone who had come to join in this momentous occasion. Two large projection screens on each end of the room began to display a slideshow of pictures dating back to the days of Nia learning how to crawl, elementary school graduation, her attendance at different friends' birthday parties over the years, family gatherings, and random pictures from school fieldtrips, events, and clubs. Uniformed waiters began to serve dinner salads and warm honey buttered rolls as the disc jockey played Whitney Houston's rendition of "I believe the children are the future" lightly in the background. Everyone looked so nicely dressed and Nia caught glimpses of her friends and family from across the room. She even saw a couple of her former teachers to her surprise.

As Nia joined the lively conversation at her family's table, she was so happy that Jihad was sitting next to her. Every now and then he would nod his head in agreement with something someone said or express a slight hint of a smile. Nia was happy that Jihad's family had come too. Nia thought her family was large, but Jihad's family was huge, and she loved that they were close knit. His sister's had embraced Nia when she and Jihad entered the hall and that meant a lot to her. She didn't really get a chance to see or spend much time around them because they attended schools in different areas, but she always had a good time when they were together.

As everyone finished their dinner, the DJ picked up the tempo and got everyone on the dance floor with the latest jams. From the babies to the oldest in the room, the party was on and poppin; the latest dance moves were in full effect and somehow a Soul Train lined had formed and everyone was calling for Nia to be the first to grace the runway that had formed. Nia knew all eyes would be on her, so she reached for her baby sister, Jasmine to join her for the birthday stroll. Jasmine was a natural born performer and she and Nia showed out as they strutted their stuff in true sisterly fashion. When they got to the end of the line, she and Jasmine hugged as Nia thought, Whew!

Glad I didn't have to do that solo. Nia was more the young philosopher; she enjoyed a good show, but she wasn't ever going to volunteer to be in the spotlight. Everyone else took turns showing off their real and imaginary dance skills and the party continued with a delicious array of food, fun, and fabulousness.

Nia walked around and greeted her guests; some of the encounters seemed to last just a few minutes while others seemed to last forever. It was great seeing people she hadn't seen in years, and she made sure that Brandon got all of it on film. These were moments she wanted captured forever. As she and some of her cousins playfully made ghetto-fabulous poses that kept onlookers in laughter hysteria, Nia noticed Jihad standing across the room speaking with a guy that she didn't recognize. Once done with the candid camera antics, she headed in Jihad's direction.

"Hey phantom," Nia teased Jihad for having a knack for staying out of the mix of all the festivities.

"What's up?" Jihad replied. "You know I fall back; get your shine on lil momma". The guy standing next to Jihad appeared to be Latin, a few years older than the couple, with a full head of thick, dark, long wavy hair that he wore neatly braided back. Jihad introduced Nia as "his girl" and the guy as "Gee". Nia awaited more details about how the two knew each other but it was clear that both guys were done with the pleasantries. Nia could sense she was interrupting so she asked Jihad what time would he be ready to leave?

"Imma walk Gee back to his car, and then it's on you".

"Okay, "she said as she walked towards the center of the room where a four-tier red velvet cake covered in cream cheese icing and beaded cake décor fit for a royal wedding was glowing with sixteen sparkly candles. As she approached, everyone began singing in unison, "Happy Birthday to You… Happy Birthday Dear Nia, Happy Birthday to You. We love you do; we love you we do."

Everyone waited for her to make a wish and blow the candles out, but Nia couldn't think of one thing to wish for because tonight all her wishes had already come true.

Nia thanked everyone for coming as they exited the banquet hall. Everyone that had arrived in the limo hopped in for the ride back to Nia's house. Nia hadn't noticed that Jihad had returned and was quietly sitting at the table where they had dined earlier. The hall's employees were cleaning the tables off and removing the décor that had truly added a magical touch to the occasion. None of the attendants had touched the table where Jihad was sitting. After Nia thanked the last few guests, she walked towards Jihad and sat in the seat closest to him. She hadn't realized it before now, but she was exhausted! They both began to speak at the same time and chuckled as Jihad gestured for her to go first. Seeing the serious look on his face, she decided he should go first.

"Was tonight everything you imagined, Jihad asked." But before she could answer, Jihad continued. "NIa, you and I have been kicking it for a while and I'm really feeling you. It ain't always easy out here for me but I want you to know that I'll always be here for you." With that, he reached into a silver gift bag and pulled out two red boxes trimmed in gold. The last few employees were almost done cleaning and were shuffling around, anticipating the departure of Jihad and Nia. Jihad opened the larger box first, and Nia's eyes widened in surprise and shock. Jihad reached into the box and pulled out a beautiful gleaming diamond tennis necklace; it had to be at least two or three carats. Most tennis necklaces NIa had seen diamonds before graduated in size from small to large but this necklace was designed with beautiful one-sized stones from beginning to end.

"Jihad," was all that Nia could utter.

Before she could really thank him, Jihad reached around her neck and clasped the gorgeous diamond necklace. Nia's dad was a certified jeweler and had always gifted his girls with the best in jewelry and timepieces, but this was different. Before she could get all sentimental and mushy with Jihad, he had already retrieved a matching bracelet from the smaller box and reached for her arm as he clasped it close. He didn't say anything more, but Nia knew that Jihad had meant what he said, he would always be there for her. He hadn't said 'I love you' but the look in his eyes told her that he did. On the way home, neither spoke to the other but Nia felt like she was in a dream that she never wanted to wake up from.

Chapter Eight

*I*t was early Saturday morning and as the breakfast aroma traveled from the kitchen throughout the rest of the house, Nia slowly opened her eyes as she stretched her arms out upon waking up. She did a double take at the sight of her right arm as the sparkling diamond bracelet seemed brighter than the sun. She quickly reached for her neck and just as she remembered, she felt a second piece of jewelry. As if mama had eyes in the walls of their room, she could hear her mom call out to the girls to get up for breakfast. Nia quickly removed both pieces of jewelry, searched the room for the silver bag, removed the two red and gold boxes, and placed the beautiful sparkling jewels in inside. She slid the bag under her bed as thoughts of Jihad and last night's events flooded her mind. She remembered Jihad giving her two expensive pieces of jewelry and now that she was sitting in the middle of her bed, so many questions began to crowd her mind. Who was Gee and what was his relationship to Jihad? How could Jihad afford the beautiful jewelry he had given her? She had worked some weekends with Pop and learned enough about fine jewelry to know that it didn't come cheap. Something deep inside told her that Jihad's after-school and weekend hours of work at the dry cleaners would fall short of the price tag for the gifts he had given her.

Jasmine rolled over after hearing mama's second call for the girls to come to the dining room and eat. The doorbell rang and as Jasmine headed to the bathroom to wash up for breakfast, she saw a glimpse of Pop standing at the door. Nia was surprised to hear her dad's voice in their house because it was rare that he came inside. Even on days that he visited the girls, he would usually blow his horn or ring the doorbell then return to his car until the girls came outside. Ms. Ali had just finished cooking breakfast and the dining table was lined with creamy cheese grits, beef bacon, salmon croquet patties, French toast, golden yellow scrambled eggs, homemade golden-brown biscuits, and several flavors of jelly.

When Ms. Ali saw Pop standing at the door she jokingly said, "You must have smelled my kitchen from across town".

Everyone who had ever eaten at Nia's house knew that Ms. Ali could've been a chef instead of a teacher. Her culinary skills could satisfy the appetite of anyone, whether the request was for vegan, seafood, or soul food, she had a knack for creating scrumptious meals that were good for the body and the soul.

So, Pop couldn't lie, "I didn't expect breakfast but I'm glad I'm right on time."

Ms. Ali and Pop were cordial in each other's presence but unless it involved the girls, they had little to discuss over the years.

"Nia!" "Jasmine!" Ms. Ali called out for the girls to join their parents for breakfast. She didn't want the food to get cold as her daughters tested her patience with their dawdling towards the table.

The family bowed their heads as Pop said the grace and everyone began to eat in silence. The girls began talking about their plans for the day and decided to check the newspaper listings for any new movies. Ms. Ali had made plans to spend her day enjoying one of her favorite pastimes, shopping at the ritzy second-hand stores. She and her two best friends, Ameerah and Tamara would travel from Miami to South Beach and then to Palm Beach just for the joy of finding the best brands for the least price. It had almost become a friendly competition between the trio. Nothing was off limits, from fine furnishings, unique artwork, couture label clothing or something unexpected. Anything Ms. Ali decided to buy but not keep would be donated to the Masjid, her Islamic place of worship.

Pop was sharing his plan to move the location of his jewelry store as the crime wave was costing him more than he could afford to run his business at a profit. He was complaining because after attending several community town hall meetings with local politicians, increased police presence had not resulted in a decrease in the burglaries occurring amongst local businesses. Before he got up from the table, he called everyone's attention towards him.

"I just wanted to stop by in person and let you lovely ladies know that you all made me so proud last night. Nia, you're growing up so fast and when we get a private moment, we are going to have a heart to heart about some things, especially your little boyfriend, his tone turning a little more serious. Jaz, you are always busy between dance classes and school, but I love how you always have your sister's back; I saw y'all strutting your stuff down the soul train line last night, he chuckled. Belle, I know I don't do or say a lot of things that I should but you're doing an excellent job with our daughters. I have a couple of friends that complain about some of the things their exes take them through, and I know I'm blessed that you don't do me like that."

Mama looked like she wanted him to shut up with the sentiments, especially given the back child support that he had yet to pay but she gave a half smile, half smirk and said "thanks." Maybe he hadn't realized it, but mama had put him their situation in God's hands a long time ago and she had no intention of blocking her blessings by trying to get even with him.

The girls walked Pop outside to his car, gave him a kiss, and waved as he drove off. They groaned at the thought of all the dishes that awaited them back in the house. Dish duty was one of the few drawbacks of big meals at home. Jaz cleared the plates as Nia began running a sudsy sink of hot water. The sisters' teamwork made the task less daunting, and they were done in less time than they had expected.

In less than thirty minutes, Ms. Ali had made a 360-degree transformation from silk scarf and house robe to a multi-color blue tunic and boot cut denim jeans which her recent cropped layered hair cut made her look younger than she was. She was ready to hang out with her girlfriends and catch up with everything that had been going on with them. Preparing for Nia's party had kept her out of the loop for the past several months, so she was looking forward to the day. She loved finding hidden treasures that were sometimes valuable and even new on occasion. As she picked up her car keys off the fireplace mantel, she reiterated the *rules* that the girls were to abide by in her absence and/or if they decided to leave the house for the afternoon.

With a few last-minute directives, the girls waved goodbye as she locked the door behind her.

Nia was glad that Ms. Ali had made an executive decision to add an additional phone line for the house in the previous weeks. Sometimes it seemed unbelievable how fast the girls were growing up and exploring various and diverse interests. Ms. Ali quickly realized that the home phone had become a major focal point for the girls, especially for NIa. Having the second phone line installed prevented her from having to become a timekeeper, referee, or extremely frustrated mom of her pre-teen and teenager.

Both girls retreated to their bedrooms as they chatted about what to do for the remainder of the day. Five years in age difference didn't seem like a big deal when you said it aloud, but an eleven-year-old and sixteen-year old's interests could sometimes be worlds apart. Nia thought about calling her friends on a three-way call to catch up and find out their plans for today, but she wasn't fond of Jasmine hanging out with her and her friends and knew Mama would frown upon her excluding Jaz. Besides, Nia quickly dismissed the thought of getting on a three-way call because everyone would begin talking at the same time, and nothing would be heard. So, she decided to catch up with them later.

Nia dialed Jihad to see what he was up to, but he said he was working. She asked if he would drive her and Jaz to the movies? He got the movie time from her and said he would be there twenty minutes before it started. Jaz and Nia showered simultaneously; NIa in the main bathroom and Jaz in Ms. Ali's master bathroom.

Both girls were glad to be getting out of the house and searched the closet that they shared for today's fashion statements. Nia had overheard Ms. Ali saying it was going to be a beautiful Miami day of 70 degrees and clear skies, so she decided on wearing her red Lacoste polo shirt, dark denim Lacoste jeans, and her white perforated Lacoste sneakers with the red trim. At age eleven, Jaz was not one for trends or labels. Sure, her classmates and friends were preoccupied with teen celebrities and what they were wearing in the world of fashion, but Jaz always seemed happy to create her own sense of style. Today, she had decided to sport her custom silver spike studded jean shorts with matching white tee shirt that she designed herself. Ms. Ali obliged Nia and bought her some additional studs so she could embellish her black converse chucks to match. Even though she was the younger sister, Nia, really admired Jaz for being original and not being afraid to walk her own path. The doorbell rang, and Nia and Jaz picked up their leather Dooney and Bourke wristlets and headed to the door. Nia checked to make sure the televisions and lights were off before setting the house alarm and locking the door. Nia could overhear Jihad teasing Jaz about all the spikes on her clothing, calling her a walking body weapon. The threesome laughed as they entered the truck and Jihad pulled out of the driveway.

Nia called Jihad from the movie theatre's telephone and let him know where she and Jaz would be waiting for him to pick them up. Jaz walked with Nia as she strolled the breezeway walking in and out of shopping boutiques and sporting stores for the latest in fashion and fancy footwork. Nia had a fetish for clothes, shoes, and handbags and was always up on the hottest couture. Her mom sometimes teased her that she had champagne taste with beer bottle money but even Ms. Ali played a part in keeping Nia photo-shoot fresh. The girls headed towards the area Jihad told them to meet him and as they approached, he was turning the corner. Nia must have had a goofy look on her face as he got closer because Jaz called her out,

"Dang, Nia, why don't you just show him all the teeth in your mouth!"

"Shut up girl!" Nia retorted as she and Jaz hopped in the truck. "Y'all hungry?" Jihad asked.

Both girls responded at once like they had been waiting all day to hear that question, "Yes".

Jihad pulled out of the loading area and headed to one of their favorite spots, Benihana, on the 79th Street Causeway. Nia gave Jihad a brief overview of the movie at which he told her that he was glad he took the rain check. A girly movie just wasn't on his agenda today. Within the next 15 minutes they were arriving at the restaurant and Jihad pulled into a parking space near the ocean view anticipating that Nia would choose to sit by the water.

The holidays were an exceptionally busy time of year at the dry cleaners, so Jihad and Nia hadn't spent much time together since her birthday bash. Nia was looking forward to lunch with Jihad. She had been thinking a lot about their relationship and was filled with questions about the expensive gifts he had given her. Her nerves were on edge trying to keep them hidden from Jaz and more importantly, from Mama.

Jaz was like a kid in the candy store as she perused the menu and ordered to her heart's contentment. Jihad and Nia sat on opposite sides of the table and Jaz sat next to Jihad. The intercostal view was peaceful and one of the reasons Nia always loved anything that happened on, near or in water. The waiter walked towards the kitchen with everyone's order and returned with shrimp tempura appetizers and lemonade for all three. Jaz had gotten up to go to the ladies' room and Jihad seemed to be in his own world as Nia called out to him twice before he responded.

"I wanna ask you a question but I don't want you to take it the wrong way," Nia said.

"Go ahead, I'm cool" Jihad replied.

"Well, I really really love my birthday gifts and I appreciate you for thinking so much of me but where did you get that kinda money? I mean, I know you work and all but ain't that much part-time money in the world. Besides, I cringe every time Jaz or mama come in the room looking for something or just to talk cause I'm hoping they don't find my new daily secret hiding spot. Nia had started out with one question but found herself rambling. Jihad, always cool, calm and collected had leaned back a little in his seat and was listening intently and looking Nia directly in her eyes. As he was about to begin, the waiter was now setting their entrées in front of each of them and Jaz put away the puzzle she had been working on since returning to her seat. Nia was happy to see their food but thought it was sure to give Jihad a reason to delay his response to her concerns. But Jihad continued as if the waiter hadn't interrupted anything,

"I told you the night of your party that it's not easy for me out here. You can't imagine the weight I carry, nor should you have to. I want you to focus on us and let me focus on everything else. You gotta decide for yourself if you trust me. I can tell you a million times that I am not going to put you in harm's way but at the end of the day, only you can decide if you're going to rock with me or not. I put a lot of thought into your birthday gifts, and I wanted to give you something that would show you what you mean to me. It's not even about the money, if it was, I could've just given you a card with some cash in it. With that, he laid his napkin in his lap, picked up his fork and began to dig into his plate of seasoned rice, shrimp, steak, and lobster with sautéed veggies on the side.

Nia still hadn't received the answers she was looking for but thought it best to fall back for now and enjoy lunch with Jihad and Jaz. Besides, even though she couldn't put her finger on whatever it was that was tugging within her, she did know one thing. She believed Jihad when he said he'd never allow her to be hurt. She believed that he loved her and that was going to have to do for now.

Jaz fell asleep on the ride home and Jihad and Nia talked about how fast the winter recess was ending. Nia had applied to several universities and for a moment she wondered what Jihad's plans were after high school. Jihad leaned his head back on the headrest as Anita Baker crooned, Giving You The Best That I Got. His eyes were focused on the road, but his mind drifted off to another world.

Chapter Nine

Nia loved the month of December for obvious reasons, it was her birth month, everyone was out of school for two weeks of Winter Recess, people tended to be happier with all the glee of writing personal Christmas wish lists and shopping for loved ones, and the great anticipation that the coming year brings. Jihad's family had an annual tradition of celebrating for the first day of the New Year. Everyone who was biological or extended family was invited to a feast fit for a small town. His mom, sisters, aunts, uncles, cousins, and on and on all showed up in jovial spirits to celebrate.

It was a wonder to behold because the party didn't just take place at the house; it took over the entire block. Nia and Jaz were invited and were welcomed by most and scrutinized by some. Of course, Nia, "the girl that had been occupying a lot of Jihad's time" was not going to go unnoticed. Nia had seen how she and Jihad's peers reacted in his presence; always acknowledging him but never invading his space. It's like he had created an invisible boundary that people just didn't step into. Being around his family gave her a more in depth understanding of how much she didn't know about Jihad. Everyone from toddlers to great aunts treated him like a young king and he seemed to take his role as son, brother, grandson, etc. very seriously.

The love between he and family was genuine and they were fierce protectors of each other. Without having asked, Jihad was interrupted during a moment of laughter with his uncles as a cousin brought him a plate piled high with his favorite foods. Without a word uttered, Jaz and Nia were also brought plates of food that made your mouth water just from looking. Jaz and Nia sat with some female family members and talked about regular teenage stuff; clothes, boys, school. They were really nice to Nia and Jaz, and it was during the conversation that Nia learned that Jihad's mom had the same birthday as she did. Nia was surprised and couldn't believe Jihad hadn't mentioned it especially since he'd attended her own birthday party. All the girls laughed it off as a guy thing and kept the conversation moving. Nia got to see Jihad move about in his natural habitat of family and close friends and this was the most relaxed he'd seemed since she'd met him. It was clear that he loved them all very much and that the feeling was mutual. Jihad checked in on Nia and Jaz from time to time at which his uncles teased him about his exaggerated concern about his girl, which was met with everyone's laughter. Jihad was a good sport about it all and continued to mix in and out of the crowd.

As Jihad walked away from Nia and his family, the silver Porsche that Jihad had escorted Nia to her party in pulled up to the gate but this time the same guy that Jihad had introduced as Gee was driving. Without a word to anyone,

Jihad left the yard and went around to the passenger side and got in the car. Gee pulled off and Nia silently wondered what the deal was between these two. Nia knew she wasn't the only person to observe Jihad's departure but no one else spoke on it so she kept her inquiry to herself. It was getting late anyway. Some of the guests had left, others were playing cards or playing dominoes as the kids were riding bikes and playing with the toys they'd received for Christmas in the yard. Jihad returned within 30 minutes, and he asked Jaz and Nia if they were ready to go home? Despite the fact that the girls were really enjoying themselves, they knew it was best to head home since school was tomorrow. They waved goodbye to everyone and promised to visit again soon.

When Jihad pulled in front of the girls' home, he told NIa to go get the gifts he'd bought her and give them to him. Nia's eyebrows rose with a look that said, "What? Why would I return *my* gifts to you?" Jihad realized how his request must have sounded to Nia and he chuckled, "Man, go get the bag, what's yours, is yours". Of course, she was surprised by this request, but she complied with very little hesitancy. Even at sixteen, Nia knew diamonds and women didn't easily part. He told her that he would pick her up after school on Monday. Nia thought, "What?" For one, he was in school himself so how would he make it to her school in time to pick her up and secondly, he knew she had a ride. Her mom was an exceptional education teacher in the high school that she attended. Nia was learning that Jihad's lack of elaboration caused her to often have to fill in the blanks of what he was saying or just wait and see what he meant. Either way, it had been a long day. She dismissed her thoughts, reached into the truck giving him a hug and kiss goodnight.

Chapter Ten

At first thought, Nia rebelled against having to attend school on the same campus that her mom worked but she didn't want to leave the classmates that she had become friends with during her middle school years. Attending the same school where your mom taught seemed like a teenager's worst nightmare but being in the same building with Ms. Ali actually had some perks. Since she didn't have her own car, Nia always had access to some wheels for lunch when she and her girlfriends chose to eat off campus, she wasn't shown any real favoritism by the other teachers but they didn't seem to hassle her like they did other kids sometimes, and it didn't hurt that her mom's good relationship with the counselors helped to ensure she was taught by some of the best teachers in the building. One of the disadvantages was that she didn't live in the same neighborhood as her classmates, and she didn't go to school with her neighbors, so she sometimes felt disconnected; always in transition between the two worlds of home and school life.

Jihad had become a loyal constant in her life and although she'd had two high school crushes before meeting him, they had dissipated before they really ever got started. One reason

Nia hadn't had a real relationship before Jihad was that her parents were extremely strict.

Just thinking about the consequences that could come from having a boyfriend was more than enough for Nia to not jump off the porch too quick. Her mom had drilled the short version of the birds and the bees speech more than she cared to remember and her dad, well he had cut up so bad one time when a male classmate called the house for Nia, she hated to imagine what he'd do if he knew she had a boyfriend. Besides her parents trying to keep tight reigns on her, Nia had little patience for the cat and mouse games she saw some of her friends go through. Her first little boyfriend, if you wanted to call it that, was Ray. As the handsome star basketball player of Nia's rival high school, the hype and fanfare were too much to keep him focused on one girl. It didn't take long for NIa to get the message and to send it right back; he was cool and all but groupie she was not.

She met the second guy, Dedric, at one of her girlfriend's birthday party. He was about 6'0 feet tall with a light brown smooth complexion and thick, black wavy hair. He had a slim build and beautiful white teeth. His smile made girls tingly inside and he knew it. It was obvious and a little embarrassing how the girls went out of their way to get close to him, but he didn't seem to take himself too seriously.

Her first impression was that he must be of Latin decent just by the dialect when he spoke. He was a comical character that made Nia laugh and any guy that can make a girl laugh has a pretty good shot at getting her attention. Nia felt all eyes on her as he approached speaking Spanish in her ear, "Hola! at the party. Coincidentally, they had both worn all white that night. Nia wore fitted white denim jeans with rhinestone details and a matching tank top that sparkled in the dark with silver shoes and matching accessories. He couldn't be missed in a white on white Adidas sweat suit with the matching all white shell toe kicks. It was no other way to say it, but he was *FINE*. Sasha had pulled NIa away from her conversation with Dedric just long enough to give her the run down on her new amigo. First of all, He had graduated two years ago from one of the most popular inner- city schools in Miami, was known for getting money in the streets, had a girlfriend that had sliced a chick's face during a fight about him, and he would probably lose interest in Nia the moment he found out she wasn't giving up the goodies as in s-e-x goodies. Nia took heed to Sasha's friendly advice but not one to run from a challenge, she returned to her cozy conversation with Dedric. NIa was far from naïve; she'd seen the game played so often; she could write the plays herself. She saw through Dedric like freshly cleaned glass. She had to admit, they did look good together but that was the extent of it. First of all, the moment he opened his mouth and she saw the meticulously polished gold grill; she knew she couldn't even introduce him to her mom. Not that Ms. Ali would unfairly judge him, but she *would* object to him dating Nia. Ms. Ali had worked twice as hard as her Caucasian counterparts during her studies at a predominately white university, dedicated her life to teaching kids of all ethnicities and abilities and had repeatedly told Jaz and Nia that fair or not, presentation was just as important as substance, especially for children of color. So, in Ms. Ali's opinion that expensive gold dental embellishment would disqualify him from any decent career and thus disqualify him from dating Nia. She and Dedric exchanged phone numbers, remained cool over the years and checked on each other from time to time.

When Nia met Jihad, she wasn't looking for a boyfriend or drama. She had witnessed firsthand how the word love could turn into a filthy four-letter word and she was content to enjoy friendships but didn't share some of her girlfriend's eagerness to become the target of some guy's fickle affections. So, as she and Jihad grew closer, it surprised her how much and how quickly he had become a major part of her world.

There was no doubt she loved Jihad; he was kind, loyal, generous, and more than anything, he made her feel safe. She was just pre-wired with hesitation because she didn't want to relive the feelings of heartbreak and abandonment that her parents' divorce had marred her with. She was young and having fun, anticipating college life, and looking forward to new experiences. She wasn't about to fall victim to cupid and the chaos he sometimes brought with him. Nia knew that other girls had tried to push up on Jihad, tempting him with things that she wasn't yet willing to give like having sex. She was scared to death of disappointing her mom and of getting pregnant. Besides some of the stories she'd heard from her friends didn't make it sound all that rewarding, especially the first time.

Chapter Eleven

Nia went to her locker to retrieve her math book for tonight's homework, the novel her language arts class was reading, *I Know Why the Caged Bird Sings* by Maya Angelou, and put her 6th period science textbook inside. She passed lip-locked couples in the hallway and waved goodbye to friends headed in different directions as she walked towards the student parking lot where Jihad said he would meet her.

She saw his truck backed into a space in the farthest corner of the rear lot and thought to herself, why in the world would he park waaaayyyy back there? She was in no mood for any additional exercise after that grueling physical education class today. Coach Davis must have had a flash back of his military days and put the class through a regiment that could be compared to boot camp training. Nia and two of her close friends had all been voted as Senior Superlatives so it went without saying that they were popular and known to hit the bullseye both academically and socially amongst their peers. However, knowing she would see Jihad today, gave Nia an extra incentive to add an extra letter *y* on her flyy-ness. She wore a fuchsia pink button up shirt with bedazzled black buttons tied at the waist revealing a little of her pecan tan complexion and sparkling metallic black jeans with a black patent belt, crystal-embellished sandals, and black and grey MCM cross body bag to match. She'd worn her black Members Only bomber jacket today in her classes, but it was blazing hot outside, so she took it off as she exited the building. Her shoulder length dark burgundy hair was spiraled curled, and she had received numerous compliments on it throughout the day.

Jihad started the engine and mumbled something about not being too late as Nia hopped in the passenger side. Nia still didn't know where they were headed and wondered why it couldn't wait until the weekend. She was lucky her mom had a faculty meeting after school today, so she was able to arrange her own transportation without much discussion.

"Where are we headed"? Nia asked? Jihad gave her a half smile and said,

"I just wanted you to ride with me; I got something to do before 5:00". With that, Jihad turned the music up to the sound of Public Enemy, leaned back, and moved his head to the beat streaming from his custom auto sound system.

The traffic on highway 826 West was gridlocked as usual for this time of day and Nia observed Jihad check his black Bvlgari sports watch several times. Jihad was always dressed nicely but he never seemed caught up on trends. His everyday wardrobe consisted of denim jeans or shorts from one urban designer or another and coordinating pullover polo shirts. He did however have a passion for footwear and watches and spared no expense on the best. Jihad switched lanes and started travelling from the carpool lane to the right, getting off at the next exit. Nia had spent the ride singing and swaying to endless hot tracks played by Miami's 99 Jamz radio station and hadn't paid attention to their route until she noticed him pull into a NationsBank parking lot and park in front of the entrance. He unlocked the glove compartment, retrieved the silver bag that Nia had returned to him last night, opened his door, and hopped out of the truck. He noticed that Nia didn't immediately follow suit, so he told her, "Come on, we're here." We gotta get in by 5". Nia, wondering why they had travelled 30 plus miles in the opposite direction of home just to go to a bank, pulled the door's lever and got out of the truck. Jihad was already holding the bank's door open for her as she walked in and waited for him. Jihad was greeted by a Latin male employee with a smile and asked how could he help Jihad today? Jihad pulled out a key ring with one bronze medium sized key on it and gestured towards the safe deposit box area and the gentleman promptly called for a manager to assist Jihad. Before entering, Jihad informed the lady that he needed an additional key and to add a name to his account. She walked off and quickly returned with a small box, pulled a signature card out and asked for Nia's identification. Nia stepped forward, pulled out her wallet and gave the lady her ID. She quietly asked Jihad what was up, but he just put his arm around her waist and signaled for her to wait as the lady completed the paperwork. In less than 10 minutes, the manager, Jihad, and Nia were on the other side of two secured vaulted doors and the banker was pulling out a draw with number 423 down. She used one key from her key ring and waited on Jihad to insert his key to unlock the large sized box. She then escorted the couple to a private room and left them alone. Jihad lifted the box's top, and Nia couldn't believe her eyes. The box was stacked row after row with large neatly rubber banded bills. She couldn't even estimate how much money was there. She just knew it was more than *a lot.* Jihad pulled the two red gift boxes from the bag and added them to the box. He then reached back into the bag and pulled out more stacks of money and added them to the box. He re-locked the box with his key and called for the manager to lock the other side. In less than 20 minutes time, Jihad had pulled Nia into a part of his world that she didn't even know existed.

As they exited the bank, the manager and security officer waved goodbye and wished them a pleasant afternoon. Meanwhile, Nia was speechless as her mind was overwhelmed with thoughts and questions. However, when Jihad asked, "You good?" instead of confronting him with her questions, she quietly replied, "yes" as they drove off.

Chapter Twelve

There was nothing typical about Jihad. Most guys his age spent their free time playing sports or girls; most times a little of both. From outward appearances he seemed like the average guy from around the way with his smooth mocha complexion, 5'9 in height, average athletic build, and fresh low fade haircut. There was just a hint of facial hair to be seen subtly announcing him coming into his manhood. And like a lot of young black men growing up in the inner city, he had seen his fair share of fast girls, fast cars, and fast lifestyles.

In a crowd of neighborhood kids, Jihad blended in as just one of the guys, but his life was far from that of a typical 16 year old. Jihad was a manager of his family's community coin laundry and had become quite savvy at customer service, laundry machine repair and money management. The visit to the bank with Jihad had clued Nia in that Jihad was unlike the average boy she attended school with whether she was ready or not, she was in store a whirlwind hood love adventure.

This blossoming young love was really an enigma to the people who knew the couple from around the way because even though Nia wasn't the kind of girl who was always on every scene, she was known for her humorous, outgoing, and no holds barred personality. Whereas, Jihad was reserved, preferably playing the background role even though his family was well known among the who's who of the movers and shakers on South Florida getting money scene. He wasn't an attention seeker and preferred to let his sisters and cousins get their *Hollyhood* shine on. In some ways the couple was like night and day. Nia being more outgoing and outspoken, he was light on words but heavy on presence. Whether it was just the two of them or a room full of people, the way he moved created a mystique about him that kept people speculating. His silent demeanor wasn't to be taken as weakness. In fact, he maneuvered through the hood like an oxymoron; edgy yet smooth. The fastest girls in the hood showed no shame or hesitancy when trying to push up on him and even though any man loves the attention, it was apparent from his lack of enthusiasm that it would take more than thighs and breast to earn his attention.

Nia's parents had drilled the 'boys and books don't mix' speech into her head so much over the years until she hadn't really looked at the guys around her as much more than friends. But Jihad's aura was like a magnet that kept drawing her closer. Initially she had whined to her friends that Jihad was way too quiet for her. She was a conversation connoisseur; always willing to strike up a conversation about anything from fashion to the increasing wave of black on black crime that was responsible for the premature ending of so many lives. So, when Nia met Jihad and he always seemed reserved and quiet, she initially thought *this isn't going to work*. But what Nia came to learn over time was that silent did not mean weak. In her home, Nia had been taught to celebrate the advocacies of men like Dr. Martin Luther King, Jr. and Minister Malcolm X. Both men had used their voices to help bring change in the lives and communities of African Americans. Though Jihad didn't talk much, it was clear that his dreams extended beyond his daily routine at his family's business and that he was a young man who wanted a life, a girl, and a hustle to call his own.

Nia's mom called out, "Nia pick up the telephone" from the other room.

Nia wasn't expecting anyone's called but she was pleasantly surprised to hear Jihad's voice when she said, "hello?"

"What's up,?" Jihad replied.

Nia caught herself smiling at the sound of his voice and quickly quit grinning long enough to say, "not much, watching tv" He asked her if she wanted to see him? And before she could get all the word 'yes' out of her mouth, she heard the doorbell as he said, "Come outside". Come outside, Nia thought? Well dang, he just knew she was going to say yes, huh? She checked herself in her bedroom mirror, slid on some sandals and told her mom she was going outside. Jihad was already standing outside his truck on the passenger side and opened the door for Nia as she approached.

She teased him by saying, "Oh so you just knew I was going to say yes, huh? What if I would have said I was busy doing something?"

Jihad had made his way back to the driver's side and replied, "I was hoping you wanted to see me too but I'm persistent. I would have kept coming back until you said yes." And with that, they both burst out laughing.

Seeing Jihad laughing out loud was a rare occurrence for Nia and she liked how relaxed he seemed around her. She hadn't mentioned the black gun pouch that she'd seen peeking from beneath his seat and she couldn't help but wonder why he would be driving around with one, especially not being legally old enough? But this was the second time that she had wanted to question Jihad but decided to chill and keep her thoughts to herself.

It was almost instinctively that she felt, questioning Jihad would force him to either lie to her or fall back from her because he didn't seem to be all that forthcoming with the intricacies of his life. She really liked Jihad and didn't want to back him into a corner or push him away. There was a lot about him she had yet to learn but she was intrigued and willing to give him a chance to see he could trust her in his own time. Besides, she couldn't put it into words but there was never a time in his presence that she felt in harm's way; if anything, when she was with him, she felt absolutely safe.

Chapter Thirteen

*S*enior year was proving to be moving faster than the speed of lightening. The anticipation that had built up over the past three years was now spilling out in many different directions at the same time. It seemed that Nia, like many of her classmates were trying to balance the excitement and activities of one of the most momentous years of their lives along with the accountability of preparing to enter the next chapter of their lives. Just thinking about SAT scores, college applications, scholarship applications, senior year festivities, rivalry football games, pep rallies, homecoming activities, senior superlatives voting, prom, part-time jobs, not to mention all the real-time homework that was still being assigned right smack in the middle of them trying to enjoy the best of these memorable moments.

Nia had entered several writing contests for college scholarship awards but when she was called over the PA system by the front office instructing her report to her guidance counselor's office, her writing entries were the last thing on her mind. Mr. Stephens, her senior counselor, had taken a special interest in Nia and some of her friends or at least it seemed that way to them. Truth be told, Mr. Stephens had a particular way with making every student feel like he or she was the most important student that he advised. As Nia entered Mr. Stephens' office, she noticed he had a serious look on his face. Mr. Stephens wasn't known as an overly social personality but today he seemed a little more reserved. Nia's mind began to race wondering if something was wrong and if so, what could it possibly be? Mr. Stephens gestured for Nia to have a seat and he began by sharing that he thought she was a very talented young writer. Nia was far from the nervous type, but she felt like there was a "but" coming somewhere in Mr. Stephens' speech. She continued to listen as he proceeded to tell her that it's not every day that he meets students who almost effortlessly write as well as what he'd seen in her works. By now Nia was silently wishing Mr. Stephens would just spit out whatever he was trying to say. As if he was reading her mind, Mr. Stephens picked an envelope from his desktop and handed it over to her. The return address label read The Dr. Martin Luther King Essay Contest with the Atlanta, GA Center For Human Rights Address. The envelope had already been opened so Nia pulled the letter out. As she read further down the letter, she could see Mr. Stephens watching her intently as she finally read the line that stated, "Congratulations, you have been awarded the third place prize for your essay entry." The letter proceeded to include that several thousand students had submitted essays from all across the United States and only three had been selected to receive a financial award for their essays. Nia looked up at Mr. Stephens who was smiling from ear to ear and even though she had just read it for herself, she almost couldn't believe what she'd just read. The letter concluded by stating that Dr. King's oldest daughter, Ms. Yolanda King, would present the scholarship award during her visit to South Florida within the next few weeks.

Nia leapt from her seat and ran around to Mr. Stephen's side of the desk. She hugged him so tight, that it wasn't until she heard his voice, that she quickly released him. Mr. Stephen's was still smiling as he congratulated Nia and continued to share that he was most confident that great things awaited her as she prepared to attend college. Nia couldn't stop thanking Mr. Stephens because it was, he that had informed her of the essay contest in the first place. Nia hugged him once more as she left his office, heading to her mom's classroom to share the great news.

Ms. Ali was not in her classroom when Nia arrived and no one on the hall knew where she was. Nia hung out for a few minutes before returning to her own class to gather her belongings and head to her next class so she wouldn't be late. She wondered where Mama could be? She was filled with both excitement and disbelief and couldn't wait to tell her mother of the awesome news!

Chapter Fourteen

Ms. Ali had been overjoyed with the news of Nia's scholarship award and had called each grandparent, aunt, and uncle to share the great news. Nia never understood how mothers wasted no time making their children's business – family business. Nia's mind was always analyzing one thing or another and she wondered was it a Black mother thing or were all mothers that way? Yes, it was all-good when the news was good but let it be bad and the news seemed to travel even faster. Nia was glad that the phone calls were received with celebratory joy, and everyone seemed just as excited as she was. Her grandmother who rarely left the comfort of her rural South Georgia town even vowed that she would not miss Nia's graduation for anything in the world.

Pop surprised everyone by showing up unannounced to take the girls to dinner to celebrate. Nia hadn't actually heard her mother call Pop, but she knew without a doubt that he had gotten the news as well. Despite her parents' inability to keep their family together, they generally were in agreement when it came to their daughters. Pop wasn't a big seafood eater, but he jokingly shared that Nia could've been a mermaid. She loved everything about the ocean. Ever since she was a little girl, she enjoyed frolicking on the seashores of

South Florida. As Pop and Jaz chatted about school, Nia's mind drifted back to a now funny childhood memory.

Nia's parents had invested in swimming lessons for both their daughters during their elementary school years at the local parks and recreation facility, but Nia had gotten herself thrown out of summer camp on the third day. Apparently, the swim coach had successfully tossed hundreds of kids into the ten feet deep end of the pool and watched as they desperately attempted to grab the long pole that he tossed out at them to deliver them safely back to the pool's deck. But when he tossed young Nia into the deep end of the park's pool, the outcome didn't quite go as planned. Nia had seen the other children get tossed in and she saw the panic and desperation as they flipped and flapped their arms in an attempt to grab the pole. She wasn't looking forward to the experience even though the other youngsters tried to reassure her that it wasn't that bad. It seemed, without warning, it was Nia's turn and just like that – she was flung into the air and into the pool's deepest end. As soon as Nia hit the water, she began flailing her arms about in attempt to reach for the extension pole. It only took a few seconds for Nia to retrieve the pole and the coach quickly pulled her towards the pool's edge so that she could return to the deck. However, this is where everything went left. Nia couldn't seem to catch her breath and she was on the verge on tears as the coach approached her. Just as the coach had tossed Nia into the water without warning, as he reached for her to see if she was okay, she grabbed his arm and bit him! She bit him so hard that he snatched his arm back and yelled,

"What did you do that for?" Nia just stared blankly at him and ran to gather her belongings from the locker room.

Although there was no break in the coach's skin, he did receive first aid treatment before returning to the pool. When Nia's mom arrived to pick the girls up, she was instructed to take Nia home and to not bring her back to swim lessons.

Mama usually could get her point across with a certain look or glance at her girls but after today's episode; Mama couldn't refrain from reprimanding Nia and releasing a few choice curse words every so often. Jazmine sat in the back seat quietly, but she couldn't help but snicker at Nia as Ms. Ali continued to question her.

"Nia, why in the hell would you bite that damn man?" "First of all, you don't know anything about him! You put your mouth on a complete stranger! Are you out of your doggone mind?" As Jazmine listened, she couldn't help but think, "Mama isn't even concerned if Nia hurt the coach." Jasmine knew her mother had never condoned or encouraged violence in their home, so she wasn't surprised at the verbal scolding Nia was receiving. Jazmine assumed that Mama wasn't overly concerned with the coach because he had reassured her that he was okay as he hurried her and the girls to the parking lot. Well, Jazmine thought, that's the end of swim lessons. Coach hadn't said that Jazmine couldn't return but it wouldn't be the same without Nia so Jazmine figured she'd learn some other time. Mama had calmed down just enough to tell the girls to go inside and get ready for dinner. And if Nia, thought that was the end of it, she was mistaken.

Mama added, "Nia, you're on punishment until I tell you different". Everyone entered the house, and each went in a different direction once inside. "Nia! Nia!" She heard Pop's voice calling her back to the present. "Girl, what is your mind on? This is my third time calling you! Come on, we're here". Nia gathered her small Louis Vuitton clutch that her mom had passed down to her and stepped out of the car. Her stomach grumbled as she anticipated the hurtin' she was about to put on this scrumptious meal of lobster, shrimp, steamed broccoli, and garlic mashed potatoes. She hoped Jaz and Pop knew what they wanted to eat because her tummy was racing with the anticipation of the scrumptious meal-to-come.

Chapter Fifteen

Jihad hadn't been himself lately; a little distant. Nia had tried calling and talking to him on more than a couple of occasions, but he only stayed on the line for a few minutes before coming up with one excuse or another to hang up. Nia couldn't put her finger on it, but something was up. She called her friend Sasha and probed to see if together, they could get to the bottom of it.

"Sasha, have you seen Jihad around?" Sasha was usually quick to help Nia get the scoop but today she seemed reluctant to answer Nia's question.

"Nah, not really, why? She replied. "Why?" when have you ever needed a reason to pour the tea, Nia retorted and what kind of answer is "not really"? Either you've seen him around or you haven't. The more Nia thought about Jihad, the more she felt uneasiness in the pit of her stomach. Something was up and in due time it would surface. Nia knew if Sasha knew anything of a serious nature, she wouldn't hesitate to tell her so if she knew something and was holding back at all about what was going on with Jihad, it either 1. was nothing major or 2. she didn't have enough details to be certain. One thing about Sasha, she didn't mind a good juicy story, but she wasn't into gossip or slander. So, if Sasha told you something, you could pretty much take it to the bank. Nia heard Jaz laughing so loudly until she began coughing which prompted her to tell Sasha she'd call her back so she could see what was so funny.

Jaz was watching *Home Alone*, and real tears fell from her eyes as she chuckled at the antics of Macaulay Culkin's character. The young character's wit and keen sense of comedic survival had Jaz tickled and for the moment Nia had forgotten about the shenanigans with Jihad. Nia decided to study for final exams since they weren't that far off. The seniors' final year of high school was quickly passing and there were only a few weeks remaining before Nia, her friends, and all of her classmates would be transitioning from the protective hallways of lifelong friends for the adventures of new experiences and friends forging into the futures they'd been preparing for. Nia's high marks had gotten her exempted from her English and Social Studies exams but unless there was a miracle somewhere with her name on it, there would be no escaping her Math and Science exams. The more Nia studied, the less she understood. She had almost given up on trying but her mother had convinced her that teachers respected the efforts of the resilient learner. Mama had paid for tutors and still Nia struggled in Math more than any other subject. Ms. Ali was a wise woman of few words. When she spoke, it behooved you to listen because she was not likely to repeat herself twice. One of her favorite sayings was "One hand washes the other and both hands wash the face." In typical teenager fashion, Nia would oftentimes dismiss Ms. Ali's words of advice but that never stopped her mom from being a constant encourager to her daughters. She was always telling them that though they had good friends with whom they shared many interests, it would not hurt them to befriend peers with contrasting academic strengths and weaknesses. Her point was that if you only surround yourself with people who share your strengths and interests, who will you be connected to in times that your needs may exceed your resources? Who will be there to help you and how will you be a help to those around you? To high school and middle school adolescents, this sometimes went way over the girls' heads, but it didn't make the message any less wise. Having friends who liked English and detested math as much as Nia, left her with very few classmates to call on when she was stuck on a complex multi-step mathematics problem. Speaking of Math, Jihad had a natural ability in Math, and just like that Nia felt a tingling in her stomach at the thought of Jihad. Nia had reached her tolerance for the unexplainable disconnect with Jihad lately and she was about to get to the bottom of it sooner rather than later.

Nia brushed her hair back into a smooth ponytail, used her favorite skin conditioner, coconut oil, to enhance the natural glow of her pecan-colored complexion and stuck her feet into a pair of rhinestone sandals before telling her mom she'd be back shortly. Nia knew that lately she had been busy with school, but she was never too busy to kick it with Jihad, so she was at a loss, trying to understand why he was handling her with a long-handled spoon. She pulled up to the cleaners where he should be this time of day and hopped out of her mom's burgundy Nissan Maxima GLE.

THORNS OF ROSES

Her first sigh of relief as she entered the coin laundry was when she caught a glimpse of Jihad wiping off the machines and countertops. At least he was where she *expected* to find him this time of day. Jihad's back was facing Nia so when she called his name, she could tell by the way he turned around that he wasn't startled but he wasn't expecting her either. She tried to read his facial expression to see if he was pleased or annoyed by her just showing up unannounced. He seemed like he had been deep in thought and was trying to collect his thoughts. "Hey, what's up Nia?

Nia thought, "This certainly isn't the greeting I was expecting" but she replied, "What's up?" Jihad's eyes gave the Cleaners a quick scan as if he were expecting someone else any minute.

Nia didn't waste time with pleasantries and asked, "Why haven't we hung out in a while, is there something you want to tell me?" She could tell from the way Jihad's jaws tightened; he didn't like being put on the spot but at this point she didn't care. She came for an explanation and didn't plan on leaving without one.

Jihad replied, "Let me finish up here and I'll meet you at your house in 30 minutes. We can go get something to eat." Nia felt like Jihad was trying to delay or stall answering her, but she also knew that Jihad wasn't about to engage her while at work, so she shrugged and replied, "Okay" as she turned and walked back to the car. She could feel Jihad's eyes on her, so she made sure she put a little extra bounce in her step as she left hoping that she wasn't losing her best friend to any of the vices that a young man was sure to encounter in their circles. Nia and Jihad had gotten passionately close but had not had sex despite the ever-present pressure from her peers to take things to the next level, Nia was so grateful that Jihad had never tried to push her past her own willingness to do so. In Nia's home, there was never a "birds and the bees" conversation. Just watching Ms. Ali work two jobs to give her girls a decent life had greatly influenced Nia's hesitance to rush into all the responsibilities that accompanied adulthood. Nia had witnessed and lived with the consequences of love gone wrong and though she really could see herself being with Jihad forever, she knew love was a gamble and sometimes no one won.

Chapter Sixteen

One of the main things Nia loved about Jihad was that he was reliable. She was super big on honesty and really hated to be lied to. She didn't know if her disdain for liars came from the many disappointments of waiting for her father to keep his promises mostly during the time of her parents' separation and ultimate divorce or if it was just an innate personality trait that she possessed. Nevertheless, Nia had little tolerance for people who lied because no matter how painful the truth was, there was something about a lie that cut you to the core.

Nia must have sensed Jihad's presence at the front door because before he could ring the doorbell, she had peaked out the window and was unlocking the heavy black iron bar door to let him in.

"You got a tracker on me or something?" Jihad jokingly asked. Nope Nia chimed but she did seem to have a sixth sense when it came to Jihad. It didn't seem weird; just unlike any other connection she'd ever felt with anyone else. Jihad hadn't been seated ten minutes before Nia jumped in "Let me ask you a question? What's going on with you? With us?" she inquired. A flicker of sadness appeared in Jihad's eyes but as Nia gazed into them anticipating a response, the look vanished. He had unknowingly allowed Nia to see his vulnerability and though she didn't know what him in such conflict had, she just wanted whatever it was to go away so he could be okay – so they could be okay. Nia had seen this look in a man's eyes before and it had made her feel helpless then and she felt helpless now. Helpless was a strange and infrequent feeling for her, and even at an early age, Nia was aware that weakness was an attribute that few respected and many exploited. Jihad returned to his usual reserved and carefree demeanor. Why did guys think that hiding their emotions was a sign of strength, Nia wondered?

"I've just been busy lately; one of the guys that helps me at the cleaners went to jail so now it's all on me."

Went to jaaiiillll? Nia questioned in a high-pitched alarmed voice. "Who? Went to jail for what? Why didn't you tell me? When did he go to jail?" Nia could see Jihad's jaws tightening.

Jihad thought to himself, "This is why I've been avoiding you…too many questions that will only lead to more questions." Jihad took a deep breath and told Nia, "Right now isn't a good time for all of these questions. "Everything is cool. So just stay cool."

Stay cool?" Who did Jihad think Nia was? She had asked him several questions and she had all night or at least until Mama chose to clear her throat signaling to end the visit, to get some answers. She wasn't being nosey, but all kinds of thoughts were racing through her mind. Nia felt a lump growing in her throat. Ever since meeting Jihad, she had "been cool" but dating him was like living in an enigma; a maze that she couldn't ever seemed to get out of. Not only did she expect some answers, she outright felt like she *deserved* them. She had been rocking with Jihad heavy and she had even tried to overlook some things that really had raised her eyebrows like how he had saved so much money? Who was the dude from her party? How could he be running his family's business but was supposed to be preparing for high school graduation? Nia was feeling all kinds of emotions running through her veins. She wanted to trust Jihad and respect his space but wasn't she in this space *with* him? She didn't want to be that girlfriend; the one who doesn't give the dude room to move or is all up in his business but when he made her his girlfriend, he also made himself *her* business. She was trying to stay cool, but she was a part of his life too and if he didn't start talking, he was about to find out she wasn't some dizzy chick that was gone sit blindly by as things unraveled around her. She hadn't had any voice in the dissolution of her parents' relationship, but this was *her* relationship, and she was not going to remain silent. Either they were all in and or all out – and now was as good a time as any to make it clear – once and for all.

Jihad had just about run out of patience with Nia and her interrogation. Damn, he had done everything in his power to show her that he was solid and wasn't gonna fold on her. Guys Jihad's age biggest dilemmas were what they were wearing to school, how to keep the multiple girls they were gaming from bumping heads or working their athletic talents as a passport out of the hood. Jihad just didn't have the patience or the time to give her a script of everything his life consisted of. One of the reasons he had fallen for Nia was that she had a way of making his chaotic world seem calm. She didn't even realize how the normalcy of her life added peace to his. Compared to the chicks from around his way, she was damn near a nerd, but her swag spoke volumes about her confidence and charisma. He knew her mom had kept her close to the nest and he liked that he didn't have to worry about her on every scene. But it was days like today that he wished she would fall back and trust that he had her back. For both of their protection, he wasn't going to give her more information than she needed to know. There was no way to answer her barrage of questions without involving her. Nia was a good girl and he intended on keeping it that way. So, for now, he shrugged off all the questions and asked Nia if she wanted to go by South Little River to get a bite to eat? He knew she wasn't about to let it go but seafood was always a welcomed distraction. She gave Jihad a look like "I know what you're doing", kissed him on his cheek, and then jumped up to go tell Mama that she and Jihad were leaving to get something to eat.

Chapter Seventeen

The school's auditorium was buzzing with exhilaration! The Senior Class of 1990 was assembled and chattering with the anticipation of what was going to be the last formal occasion and greatest accomplishment of their school years – high school graduation. Nia and her friends were huddled up with so much excitement that although they were each bursting with comments, not much listening was going on. Amid all the hoopla, Nia and her friends felt the pang of separation that was sure to follow the last momentous highlight that they would share as childhood friends. Some were headed to the military, others chose various colleges and universities, some for one reason or another, would head directly into the work force to begin their lives as young adults.

The sound of Mrs. Knighton's voice blaring through the auditorium's speakers disrupted the students' thoughts and conversations and called their attention towards the front stage area. "Students, we have less than 2 weeks to prepare for one of the greatest accomplishments of your lives – the commencement of your high school graduation. This is no light task, and it will take the cooperation, participation, and maturity of each of you to help make this day one you will forever treasure". The senior class officials are distributing pertinent information and it is imperative that you and your parents read and follow the instructions explicitly. Today, you will receive your cap and gown packages along with the number order in which each of you will line up. Your names will be called in accordance with your assigned number so please do not change the order as it will negatively impact the principal's announcement of your name as you cross the stage."

Nia hadn't really thought about it until now, but she realized that her name would be one of the first to be called after the top five percent of the class. She was so close to the next chapter of her life and ready or not, she was about to embark on an adventure of new goals, new friends, but hopefully the same love with Jihad. "Jihad" Nia thought to herself. She had no doubt that he was down for her and wanted to be with her, but he also had made it clear that they were parts of his life where she was not welcomed.

Mrs. Knighton's voice interrupted Nia's thoughts as Mya nudged her,

"Aye, let's go get in line to pick up our cap and gown packages." Nia pushed Jihad to the back of her mind, and replied, "Sure, no better time than the present" giving Mya a quick hug.

Mya asked, "What was that for?"

Nia hugging her again, saying, "I don't know why you want to be a Bethune Cookman Wildcat but I'm going to miss you so much." The girls had known each other since 9th grade when Mya came to the school as a magnet student. Mya was one of the brightest students at the school and she was also hilarious and fun to hang out with. The two young ladies were about to transition from high school besties to college rivals as Nia headed to thee Florida A & M University to become one of a proud legion of distinguished Rattlers. Though both girls had been accepted to several universities, their hearts had been set on attending Bethune and FAMU, respectively.

By the time the girls joined the hundreds of other students in line waiting to pick up their orders, the auditorium had become more festive than the homecoming game.... the varsity cheerleaders and school mascot were on stage keeping the hype going and students were passing around their yearbooks to get signatures. Flashes from cameras could be seen all throughout the large room and the laughter and chatter of the senior class was something Nia didn't ever want to forget.

Her mom and teachers had warned the students upon entering high school to work hard and enjoy the journey but somehow along the way, the young adults had just wished for the day high school would be over – homework, labs, and lectures had caused them to forget that the clock was winding down on some of the best days of their lives. Now as they tried to hold on to this moment in time, it was slipping quickly like sand through an hourglass and the countdown was real.

Nia heard the chirp of her beeper and searched the bottom of her large bucket Louis Vuitton handbag to retrieve it. Nia was a little startled to see Jihad's number displayed across the small screen because he knew she was in school. Nia quickly ended her chat and told her friends she'd catch up with them later as she hurried to the counselor's office to call him from Mr. Stephens' phone in the counselors' suite.

"Hello, may I speak to Jihad?" Nia asked the little girl that had answered the phone.

"Jihaaaadddd, your girlfriend wants you."

Nia smirked while listening to the exaggerated manner that the child had called Jihad's name. She could hear him laughing and telling someone,

"Lexi is too grown." "Yeah, Jihad said into the phone."

"Hey what's up? I'm still at school, Nia informed him, as if he didn't know."

"Are you going straight home after school because I gotta talk to you about something?"

Nia, thought for a quick second and even though she had wanted to go by the mall to look for the required black outfit for graduation, she could do it another day. "Sure, I can. What time are you going to come by? "

Jihad glanced down at his Cartier Tank watch and replied, "I'll be there at five".

With that, he ended the call and left Nia wondering what could be so important that Jihad wanted to see her in person and within a few hours?

Chapter Eighteen

The sun shone brightly through the bedroom window's blinds, subtly waking Nia from her restless night of sleep. Is it possible to wake up tired? Nia's head had a dull ache and her body felt heavy with fatigue. Her mind had taken her on a roller coaster ride of memories during the night and as she opened her eyes, she felt a salty teardrop hit her bottom lip. Today was one of the biggest and most anticipated days of Nia's life and yet she felt a much-needed purging. Nia had unwittingly taught herself to wear brave smiles even when life seemed hardest to get through. But in this moment, she reflected and realized that for more than the past four years, she had fought silent, emotional battles to keep it together. She was excited. She was prepared. She was tired.

Just around the time that Nia entered high school, a relentless criminal, had managed to thrust Pop's Liberty City African Clothing and Jewelry business into unexpected national limelight and public debate. Pop's business had suffered too many burglaries to count and had nearly collapsed his inventory and profits. Pop and a few other local businessmen had desperately petitioned to the police department and commissioner's office to create a more stringent police task force to canvas the inner city business district. However, it seemed the more tactical law enforcement became, the more determined criminals were on terrorizing local businesses and the crime wave continued.

Pop's plight to save his business and provide for his family led to his one-man engineering of what he hoped would deter the ever- present threat of criminal mischief. He created a gate-like apparatus that he wired with electricity. He had brilliantly created a deterrence that was designed to keep the criminals out. Pop had secured the self- made security device over the hole in the ceiling that the crooks had torn thru to gain access to the shop. Prior to leaving the shop for the night, Pop had plugged in the electrical cord and exited after locking the shop. Pop had survived the Vietnam War and had no intention of being a helpless victim in his own community.

But when the phone rang that morning, no one in the Ali household was prepared for the tragic news that came rolling off the caller's tongue. "Come now! Come to your store NOW," yelled the caller. Apparently, Mr. Ali's self-made crime deterrent had electrocuted an in progress burglar. As Mr. Ali repeated the callers' words to Momma, his eyes seemed to go vacant. He didn't know what to think. Surely, his invention wasn't strong enough to KILL. Was it? The caller didn't identify himself and Pop hadn't thought to ask as he tried to comprehend what was being said. "A man was dead in your store." Dead. Ms. Ali had awakened the girls from their slumber to let them know she and Pop had to leave but would be back. She instructed them to not open the door or answer the telephone for anyone. The girls were still half sleep but they both understood that whatever was going on was serious enough to pull both their parents out of their home in the wee hours of the morning. Momma gave each daughter a kiss on her forehead before following Pop out of the house as he drove to the store. The ride seemed long as they rode in silence. Momma's mind was racing because she couldn't understand how in the world had someone *died* in the store during the night? Momma had no idea that Pop had created his own security mechanism or that their lives were about to be turned upside down.

As Mr. Ali approached the 62nd block of N.W. 7th Avenue, the red, blue, and white flashing lights of police cars and fire trucks hindered his view of the store. The yellow and black police tape confirmed what he had been told over the phone; his store was not only a crime scene but whoever had gotten into the shop had met an unexpected end. Mr. and Mrs. Ali got out of the car and walked about a block before they approached an officer who held his arm out to block their entrance. Mrs. Ali could see Pop's temples flaring on the side of his head, so she spoke up before this situation went from bad to worse.

"Sir, the store involved in last night's incident belongs to my husband."

The officer's physical demeanor changed instantly. He quickly responded by lifting the police tape and ushered both Mr. and Mrs. Ali to another gentleman. The detective introduced himself to both Mr. and Mrs. Ali and then asked Mrs. Ali to have a seat on a nearby bench as he interviewed

Mr. Ali. Mrs. Ali was close enough to see them both talking but too far to hear what was being said. However, within minutes whatever was said couldn't have been good for Mr. Ali because she saw a uniformed officer approach and place handcuffs on his wrists behind his back. Mrs. Ali quickly jumped up and ran towards him before anyone could stop her. As she was trying to process all that Mr. Ali was rattling off, she saw a gurney with a body covered by white sheets being rolled out of the shop. Pop was kneeling down to sit in the back of the police car and before Mrs. Ali could say another word, the car drove off with flashing lights but no siren. Mrs. Ali stood in dismay as the police car drove completely out of sight. The detective's gentle touch on her elbow brought her back to the moment as he explained it would take several hours before Pop would be processed and offered her a police escort to follow her back home. It seemed that this ordeal had been going on for countless hours but when she checked her watch, she realized that It had been less than one hour. In just that short amount of time, the already crowded street had tripled with onlookers, news journalists, and crime scene specialists. Mrs. Ali thanked the detective but decided not to draw any additional attention to herself. She maneuvered through the crowd of people to the car and rested her head on the steering wheel before pulling off and heading home to her girls.

By the time Mrs. Ali arrived home, the sun was up, the girls were almost dressed for school, and before she could sit them down and explain the unexplainable, she called her job to let them know that she would not be in today. Nia overheard Momma talking to her job and the other person on the other line must have asked was everything okay because Momma replied, "No everything is definitely not okay." With that she hung up the phone and called the girls into the living room.

Before Momma could speak, Jaz asked, "Where's daddy?" and though Nia couldn't recall the last time she'd seen her mom cry, she sat in silence as the tears fell from Momma's eyes. The girls listened intently and tried to comprehend what Momma was saying through the steady streaming tears and crackling of her voice but somehow what was clear to them was that a man had died in Pop's store by some contraption that Pop created and now he was in jail until Momma found out if he would be eligible for a bond. The only good news that came from Momma's news was that they were not going to school today because Momma honestly didn't know what the rest of the day would look like.

Within the next two years, Pop's picture had been on local and national television news and magazine covers. Some of the headlines were favorable calling Pop a local frustrated hometown hero for stopping a would-be burglar once and for all. Other headlines portrayed Pop as a violent vigilante that had taken matters into his own hands. Not hundreds, but hundreds of thousands of people were debating if Pop would face murder or manslaughter charges for the life that his "booby trap" had snuffed out. Pop had made appearances on the national talk shows of Larry King Live, the Oprah Winfrey Show as well as many others. His case was so popular that a popular South Florida attorney represented him pro bono;

there was no way Pop could ever have afforded him otherwise. Eventually a book was written about it and a movie deal was on the table. While Pop was being shuffled in and out of limousines from one talk show to another, Momma was working, holding the family down. The Ali household had endured a lot, but this situation added more pressure than the family could bear. Momma didn't have it in her to abandon anyone when they were down but when Pop finally had his day in court and was acquitted of all charges, Momma proceeded with the divorce that was already in motion prior to this tragedy.

This was how Nia's freshman year of high school had begun and to say it wasn't easy was an understatement. Looking back, it seemed like a lifetime ago but in actuality it had only been a few years. The chaos dissipated when Pop moved out and Mrs. Ali struggled to regain some sense of normalcy for her daughters. There was never any doubt that Momma and Pop didn't love each other but sometimes love just wasn't enough.

Nia slowly stretched her legs and arms as far as she could and slowly pulled herself out of bed. Today was a big day; her big day and though she would miss Jaz, Momma and Pop, she was filled with excitement of what life away in college was expected to deliver. Today was the big day, Nia was not only graduating high school, Nia was graduating childhood situations like domestic violence, two divorces, and the chaos that the criminal charges against her father had created and had all been beyond her control.

Chapter Nineteen

*A*s Ms. Ali's car entered the Miami-Dade County Auditorium's parking lot, Nia's eyes stretched wide as she read the large white banner with red bold block letters that read" WELCOME **CORAL GABLES SENIOR HIGH SCHOOL CLASS OF 1990".** Mama was grumbling about the girls taking too long to get dressed and now they would have to be patient as she searched for a parking spot in the already crowded lot. Nia's eyes raced as she searched for her friends as if she would be able to recognize anyone in the sea of white caps and gowns that had spread from one end to the other.

As Momma slowly pulled into the parking space, she reminded Nia of the designated meeting spot for all of her family after the graduation. As a faculty member, Ms. Ali would normally be assigned a teacher-duty during commencement exercises, but it went without saying that she would get to enjoy all of today's festivities from the audience alongside all the other proud parents and attendees. Momma had included detailed meeting time and location information in the invitations because she knew from past experiences that once the graduates crossed that stage and exited the auditorium, it could be almost impossible to get everyone assembled in one spot at one time.

It was bad enough that Momma and Nia had worked diligently for weeks soliciting, as many unneeded graduation invitations from faculty and students as possible. Momma joked that it would be easier to get into the White House than these high school graduations. And even after coming up with a few extras, unfortunately, the space was very limited.

Momma and Jaz waved to Nia as she enthusiastically sashayed off to join the group of graduates. As the pair entered the auditorium, Momma's eyes darted around the room to catch a glimpse of the rest of the family. Jaz' voice squealed out in a high-octave pitch, "Graaaandddmmaaa" and Momma knew her surprise was out of the bag. It had taken everything in Ms. Ali to not to mention that Grandma Lynn was coming to Miami for Nia's graduation. Everyone knew that Grandma was no fan of airplanes and rarely left her hometown unless there was a family emergency or the death of a loved one required her attendance. Jaz couldn't believe her eyes. They hadn't seen their grandma since last summer when she and Nia visited for their normal two weeks' vacation in the country. In Jaz' haste to run and hug grandma, she totally missed Uncle Troy's smiling face. He wasn't her blood uncle but, in the country, everybody was kin one way or another and he had happily offered to drive Grandma Lynn to Florida for the big day. He stood up to hug Jaz and told her how happy he was to see her. Uncle Troy kept the crowd of family laughing about the drive down with grandma. She kept on insisting that he "slow down' even though he swore he was going the speed limit.

"Grandma insisted, I don't care about no speed limit, you better slow down to MY heart's limit."

The family's laughter must have been contagious because even the strangers seated near them had begun to laugh along.

The auditorium's lights flickered on and off signaling that the program was about to begin. The audience settled down and everyone that showed up for Nia's big day couldn't wait to cheer her on. Dr. Willis approached the podium and asked all attendees to stand as the school's Color Guard led in the Pledge of Allegiance. Immediately following, the program followed as written, the welcome, introduction of honorary guests, the class president, salutatorian, and valedictorian each spoke words of celebration, encouragement, and hope for a great future. Nia and her fellow classmates sat anxiously in their seats as the last of the speakers shared sentiments of accomplishment and charging this graduating class of becoming world changers.

"Today each member of the Class of 1990 may proudly take your place in society as a world changer. You have successfully completed the courses of preparation. Today as you accept your high school diploma, let this be the beginning of new goals, new heights, and accomplishments. May your hands do great works, your heart love many people, and your head create solutions to problems so that the world is a better place because you have lived." Dr. Willis completed his speech with these words and on cue the Class of 1990 rose to their feet. The school's orchestra played the class song, as the students marched towards the designated area to begin the graduation procession. Nia's heart was beating so fast she felt like she was going to faint. She second-guessed her choice of five inch heals but of course it was too late for it to make a difference. Oh well, she thought, she was gonna rock these bad boys across the stage like she was born wearing heels!

"Cameron Abelman", "Thomas Ackerman", "Alexis Addison", the principal continued to call the students' names as they crossed the stage; "Nia Ali" Nia heard loud whistles, her name being yelled out, and cheering from the audience as her family erupted with celebration as she strutted across the stage to receive her high school diploma. Nia's smiled from ear to ear as she shook Mr. Anderson's hand and received her diploma. She was beaming with happiness. In this one moment, everything was as close to perfect as it had ever been. The only thing missing was Jihad could not attend but Nia couldn't let that dim all that was good right here; right now. Dr. Willis continued calling off the list of over 700 students as each one had their moment to receive their greatest accomplishment to date and return to their seats, "Jalesa McMillian", "Aaron Newberry on and on until he got through the last of the Ws. It is with great pride that I present to you today's graduating of class Coral Gables Senior High School." Dr. Willis said with authority and excitement. By now all of the students that had returned to their seats were standing, jumping, hugging and screaming with joy! The energy in the auditorium could not be contained and though difficult to keep order, the aisle assistants had to ensure that each row was dismissed one by one for everyone's safety. Nia couldn't believe it! She had cheered for her friends and classmates as they had received their diplomas and now as they all eagerly anticipated joining each other in the lobby and outside. Parents and guests were buzzing around with arms full of flowers, balloons, cards, and other gifts for the graduates.

As Nia exited the auditorium, her eyes darted around searching for her family. Like the other graduates, she was torn between hugging classmates and searching for her guests. She thought she spotted her Aunt Peaches across the way, so she pressed through the crowded lobby in her direction. But what she saw next stopped her in her tracks. Big gold glitter letters that spelled out N-I-A were spelled but as she tried to see who was holding them up, she spotted the last person she expected to see… Jihad!

"What are you doing here?" "You said you had to work today!" Nia playfully scolded Jihad as she bubbled over with joy. By this time Nia's entire family had joined the twosome and just when Nia felt today couldn't get better, she ran to hug Grandma Lynn. She almost knocked Grandma Lynn over as she hugged her so tight! "Grandma! You came!!!!! Momma, Pop, and Jaz all hugged Nia in celebration. Nia called out to this friend and that friend to take pictures with her, and her family and she obliged in their photo requests as well.

Hugs, congratulations, and photos continued for another 20 to 30 minutes and then Momma gave everyone a time-check so that they wouldn't be late for Nia's graduation dinner party. Getting out of the parking lot was definitely a buzz killer but there was only one-way out of the crowded lot. Nia asked Momma if she could ride with Jihad to the Rusty Pelican, the ocean front upscale eatery where Momma had reserved the patio area for today's festivities. But before Momma could answer, Jihad interrupted, "I can't go to the restaurant. I didn't lie when I said I had to work but I just didn't want to miss you do your thang today. I'll get up with you later, I gotta get back to the cleaners." Jihad could see the disappointment in Nia's eyes, but it was what it was. He gave her a hug and whispered something in her ear that made her giggle. With that, he waved bye to Momma and Jaz and headed to his car. If Nia had felt disappointed, it quickly vanished. She was so happy that Jihad had made a way to attend her graduation because she knew when it came to his money, there wasn't much that came before his grind. She clicked her seat belt and leaned back in the car as Momma and Jaz took pleasure in contemplating the scrumptious menu that would soon be set before them.

Chapter Twenty

Nia sat on her twin size dormitory bed and inhaled the essence of officially being a Florida Agricultural and Mechanical University freshman. Nia had arrived in the Tallahassee International Airport just two days after graduation alone and ready to experience the first chapter of young adulthood. Momma had informed Nia that if she waited until the fall semester, she would happily escort her to the university's campus because Momma's work schedule didn't end until a few weeks after the seniors graduated. The only options were Nia could go alone now or wait until the end of summer when Momma would be able to go with her. The thought of leaving home for the first time alone probably would have rattled the average seventeen year old but not Nia. She had a level of confidence that gave her an untamed sense of fearlessness. Besides, the campus was not new to her; she had visited several times during her high school years. Her mother's good friend and co-worker, Mrs. Allen had a sister that lived in Tallahassee who agreed to pick Nia up from the airport and help her get settled in on campus. So, in the spirit of "It takes a village to raise a child", Mrs. Ali prayed with her firstborn the morning of her departure, shared some words of wisdom and guidance, and encouraged her to forge forth in faith and excellence.

"Nia, you have made me as proud as any mother could be. Receiving your high school diploma, staying out of trouble, and pursuing higher education is more than enough reason for me to trust you with this next step. Of course, I wish you'd have chosen to wait until I could accompany you to college, but I know you have the heart and head to take this next step without me. Just know if you ever have a question, a doubt, or feel hesitant about *anything,* always pray about it no matter what it may be and trust that God will lead you in the right direction. I'm always a phone call or plane ride away." With that, Momma helped Nia load the trunk of clothing and necessities that she would take to Tally for the next three week summer session and headed to the airport.

College life was everything that Nia had imagined and then some. Life away from home gave Nia independence, exploration, new friends, intriguing professors, and plenty of time to enjoy the freedom of being away from home. Some of the girls were so excited to be away from the watchful eyes of their parents, they had to be reminded by the resident assistants to pace themselves. Some of them had mocked Nia for even considering staying in a long-distance relationship but she wasn't hearing it. In fact, she had earned so many frequent flyer miles traveling back and forth from Tally to Miami that she quickly racked up discounted and free tickets. She was in Miami with Jihad so much until most times Momma nor Pop knew she was there.

"You miss me?" was how Jihad started his invitation for her first visit since leaving Miami after graduation.

"Of course!" she replied without hesitation, which was the absolute truth! Ms. Ali had come to Tally when her school year ended and made sure Nia was adjusting well in her new endeavors, so Nia hadn't returned home between the summer and fall recess. With her first two semesters completed, Nia was looking forward to going home for winter break Jihad didn't have to convince her to take the first available flight out of Tally to the Miami International Airport. Just thinking about seeing Jihad again sent a tingle through Nia's body. There was definitely no shortage of talented, intellectual, diverse and handsome young men on FAMU's campus and Nia had met some cool people both male and female since her arrival but the thought of dating someone else never crossed her mind. Nia had made many friends across the campus, but her heart was with Jihad. When asked if she was seeing someone, Nia hesitated to answer. Not because she was ashamed or deceitful but because most of her peers would laugh at the thought of a long-distance relationship. They didn't think Nia or Jihad would be able to resist the temptations of the distance and time away from each other. Nia's honesty was often mocked and even some family members had expressed doubt in the twosome's ability to beat the odds of a long-distance romance. Mocked or not, Jihad had always kept it one hundred with Nia and she had never given him reason to doubt her, so they continued to rock with each other and block the naysayers out.

As Nia exited the airport doors, the South Florida air seemed to let her know she was home. Her eyes raced up and down the incoming traffic searching for Jihad's truck. She nearly jumped the curb into the street when she was startled from the back and picked off her feet. Jihad! she squealed with surprise and joy. She had given him the time of her arrival, but she hadn't expected the greeting that she received. Traffic is always gridlocked at the airport, so she never expected him to do anything other than pick her up from the curb. She hugged him so tight until another passenger trying to pass interrupted them.

Jihad had grabbed Nia's bags and she wrapped her arm around his arm. She tingled inside at the thought of being home with him again. Acclimating to the culture and expectations of collegiate life had kept Nia busier than she had realized and though she and Jihad had talked on the phone multiple times a day, nothing compared to this first reunion of many to come. She was observing him in every way from his confident stride to the unfamiliar cologne he was wearing. She leaned into him and though it was making it a little difficult for him to carry her bags with ease, he didn't complain because he had missed Nia just as much.

Chapter Twenty-One

The twosome bopped their heads to the R & B jams on the CD that was booming through the custom speakers of Jihad's truck. The energy was different than before Nia had left for college.

Nia couldn't distinguish if it was because of the accuracy of the old cliché, "distance makes the heart grow fonder" or if even though it had only been a few months, they were "older".

Nia reclined her seat as her thoughts drifted. She thought about how she and Jihad had shared several milestones such as her Sweet 16, senior prom, and high school graduation but the unspoken milestone of taking their relationship to the "next" level had never been fully addressed. Sure, they had been intimate as their curious hands explored each other's half-clothed warm bodies, quenching each other's thirst for connection with long, wet, lingering kisses but they had always stopped short of surrendering to their elevating rising body temperatures and intense heart rates just before sensuality flowed into sexuality. Nia had never made a pre-determined declaration that she wasn't going all the way, but Jihad must have sensed Nia's hesitancy and chose not to push pass her comfort level. Jihad could have sex with any number of girls, in fact there was always some sack-chaser willing to 'lay her bob down' to get next to a money-go-getter. Nia's didn't know why she had stopped Jihad because it wasn't about lack of trust or love. Despite the heartbreaking stories of some of her high school classmates and friends that resulted in tears of disappointment after having sex with the "one" only to discover the feeling wasn't mutual from the guy's perspective. Jihad had never pressured Nia beyond her own comfort level, and he had more than demonstrated that he really rocked with Nia. It was really hard to articulate because on one hand there's the power and purity of love and yet street culture had taught her to beware of wolves in sheep's clothing. At some point everyone learns that it's not your enemies but those closest to you that do the most harm. One of Grandma Lillie's comical quotes crossed Nia's mind, "at some point, you gotta shit or get off the pot". Just imagining Grandma Lillie saying that in her southern dialect was enough to make Nia laugh out loud. Nia was more than ready to give her all to Jihad; she just had to make sure she was ready for the good, bad or ugly that could come with her decision. Jihad glanced at Nia as he pulled the whip in the valet lane. Two uniformed young guys opened Jihad and Nia's car doors at once. Jihad took the ticket he was handed, and Nia intertwined her fingers into his as they walked away.

The warm golden honey colored sand slipped through Nia's perfectly white pedicured toes as she lay her head on Jihad's triceps. She didn't know if she was over hyping Jihad, but he sure seemed a little different – he had always been confident, but he walked a little taller, spoke with more assurance; Nia was falling more in love with the man he was becoming. The sun was setting in vibrant hues of yellow and red that it reminded Nia of strawberry lemonade. Jihad and Nia had feasted at the waterfront eatery, Oasis, and Nia was so stuffed from the lobster entrée that she could feel her eyes getting heavy with fatigue. She'd always thought it a cultural joke about eating and getting the 'itis' but it was true that a good meal just seemed to relax her.

Jihad asked Nia if she was up for a surprise and with usual poker face, he lit up as he shared a slight grin. Even as he awaited the answer, he would bet money that he knew was coming.

"I'm always ready for a surprise that includes you," Nia replied, and she meant that in every way. There was a glimmer in Jihad's eyes that intrigued Nia even more. She didn't know what the night had in store, but she couldn't think of any place else or any other person she'd rather be with. Jihad and Nia crossed the street that led back in the direction of the Oasis but instead of giving the valet ticket to the car attendant, Jihad kept walking and Nia followed as they entered the double doors of five star hotel also named Oasis. Nia assumed that maybe Jihad had to use the restroom or make a phone call but when he kept walking towards the gleaming mirrored elevator doors, she paused and looked up at his face. He repeated the question that he'd asked her when they were on the beach, "Are you up for a surprise tonight?" This time, Nia didn't respond verbally but she gently squeezed his hand, which was holding hers and continued to follow his lead.

Jihad inserted the hotel room key in the elevator's access slot and gently wrapped his arm around Nia's lower back. An automated female voice announced each floor, "Floor Twenty-four, five, six, seven, eight… 'Geesh', Nia thought, as the elevator climbed to the penthouse level on the thirtieth floor. When the doors opened, Nia couldn't believe her eyes. There was a trail of white rose petals with tall white glass vases with floating white candles. The room was completely dark with the exception the candlelight and moonlight that softly peeked through the wall of windows that spanned from the floor to the ceiling. As Jihad led Nia to the suite's living room, Nia wondered if Jihad could hear the fast, pounding sound of her heartbeat. Nia was overcome with anticipation and nervousness. She didn't know how long Jihad had been planning this or who, if anyone helped him put this surprise together but she was over-the-moon that he had taken such care with welcoming her home from college. Nia loved Jihad so much and even though the odds were against them being in a long distance relationship and all, Nia felt it deep down that this was everything she believed it to be. Jihad was complex in that he was not a man of many words; he didn't spend time trying to impress Nia or anyone else for that matter, he just seemed to be everything to everybody in his immediate circle. Without realizing it, Nia was suddenly saddened by all the weight that Jihad seemed to carry on his shoulders.

The sensation of his warm breath gently tickled the hairs on her neck and snapped Nia back into the moment as she felt a tingle slowly trickle from her neck all the way down between her inner thighs. His breathing had intensified, and Nia's heart felt like it was going to jump right out of her chest. She kept thinking to herself, "Be cool, Jihad's got you!" Nia didn't see Jihad turn the sound system on, but she heard the slow love ballads of Luther Vandross crooning through the speakers. Nia thought she would literally pass out! She was trying to take in all that Jihad had done to make this moment beautiful. His cologne was intoxicating, and his hands were strong yet gentle. Luther must have known exactly what this felt like when he sang melodies that were melting Nia at this point.

The rhythm of Nia's hips moved in perfect harmony with the passionate thrusting that Jihad was putting on her. She had replayed how she thought her first time making love would be so many times. She almost giggled out loud at the awkwardness she had imagined. But there was nothing awkward about being here with Jihad and as tiny beads of sweat formed on her forehead, she went from a scared and anxious girl to a fully engaged and passionate woman. She was fully aroused, giving Jihad everything, she had, physically, emotionally, and mentally. He was so attentive to her lean, slightly curvy body in every way. He had slowed down just long enough to question if she was okay but when she tightened her grip on his muscular back and pulled him in deeper, he knew she was more than okay. Jihad, he lifted her left leg and rolled her over on top of him. Nia was now gazing into his eyes as she lifted her body onto her tippy toes and rode him like a see saw. The sweet aroma of her fragrance filled the air as she gyrated and flexed her vaginal muscles around his hardness. Their heartbeats and moans had become one and moistness of Nia's center was making Jihad have to check his gangsta so as not to let out the awkward sound she was bound to pull out of him with the hypnotizing way she continued to wind her body while pulling him deeper inside.

After the initial pain of Jihad's hardness breaking her virginity, Nia melted under the firmness of his caress and the wet kisses that covered her body. His hands perfectly navigated every inch of her soft melanin colored skin as he pursued her with pressure and passion simultaneously. Nia couldn't describe or resist this feeling even if she tried. Remaining a virgin throughout high school was not an easy feat considering all the constant peer pressure to "do it". Two things had heavily influenced Nia's ability to keep her legs closed to the hormonal male suitors that had their best shot for the goodies. Just thinking of Ms. Ali and her endless speeches about boys, sex, babies and diseases was enough of a deterrent. But even beyond the overwhelming influence of her mother, Nia just always wanted her first time to be with someone she connected with on more than a physical level. Now as she lay sprawled out across the bed with her feet dangling from the edge and her head upon Jihad's chest, Nia drifted euphorically to sleep to the rhythm of his heart beating next to hers.

Chapter Twenty-Two

Nia was awakened to the soft humming sound of the electronic draperies retracting to let the bright morning sun in. She stretched her lean body as far as it would reach and rolled over to the empty space where Jihad had fallen asleep the night before. Nia was usually a pretty light sleeper, but Jihad had managed to get out of the bed without waking her. Her mind replayed last night from the airport to the beautiful candle lit penthouse suite and she almost couldn't believe that she had actually had sex, made love, done the nasty or whatever you wanted to call it, for the first time. Nia lay still as scenes from the previous evening replayed in her mind. Ironically, Nia had felt that she and Jihad had made love mentally many times before, but they had never consummated their relationship with sexual intercourse.

Jihad exited the shower, still damp with a white towel wrapped around his waist. Without realizing it, Nia began blushing at him so hard until Jihad jokingly said, "If I knew you were going to wake up this happy, I would've stayed in the bed". "Ha ha ha" was all that Nia could muster up as a comeback. Usually, she was quick-witted but realizing that Jihad was aware of her being on cloud nine had somewhat embarrassed Nia. She must've looked like the virgin she had been the night before to be standing there cheesing from ear to ear. She'd been grinning hard enough to make her cheeks sore. She silently *wished* he had stayed in the bed a little longer. There was something about the rhythm of Jihad's heartbeat that gave Nia the confidence to explore her sensuality uninhibited. She wanted to please him in every way, and she intended on doing just that. Nia felt so safe with Jihad. He wasn't very conversational, but he was an excellent communicator, if that makes sense? Jihad instinctively knew what made Nia tick and he had a quiet, calm way of reassuring her which is something she would never openly admit but she definitely needed and appreciated it.

"Nia…. Nia", Jihad's voice called Nia back from her private thoughts. "What's up?", Nia stuttered as she tried to regain her composure. "What are your plans for today 'cause I've gotta get back to the cleaners?" Prior to leaving Tallahassee, Nia told Ms. Ali that her flight would arrive this evening at 7:56 p.m. so since she had a full day before she was expected to arrive home, she decided to hang out by the rooftop pool since Jihad had requested a late check out, then stop by the mall to pick up a nice gift for Jihad. She couldn't think of anything that he couldn't do by himself, but she wanted to show her appreciation for making last night so beautiful.

Jihad could see that Nia was in no rush to leave the luxurious hotel so he called his cousin to pick him up so that Nia could use his car when she was ready to leave. Jihad seemed unusually relaxed for a change and that made Nia feel good. She didn't know how someone Jihad's age managed the pressure of having so many people depend on him in so many different ways. He always seemed to have a family or family-business obligation or task that required his attention so just to see him chillin', relaxing made Nia happy. She realized that Jihad had put a lot of thought into her arrival and their first night together. She kept thanking him with hugs and kisses. He shrugged it off like she was making too big of a deal of his romantic side, but she could tell that deep down he was happy that he'd made her happy.

"Heyyyyyyy girlllllll," Sasha squealed into the phone. Nia's face lit up at the sound of her friend's voice. They hadn't spoken often since they left Miami to attend colleges in different states, but they did write to each other a time or two. Nia instantly missed seeing and talking to Sasha and quickly asked, "What are you doing 'cause I'm at the Oasis Hotel for the next few hours and thought we could hang out by the pool?"

"Ooaasssis Sasha said slowly with a playful dramatic drawl. I would ask you to tell me how you ended up in paradise this morning but that would slow me down from getting dressed. Of course, I want to hang out with you *and* get all of the scoop while I'm there! See you in about 30 minutes!"

Jihad had returned to the room and Sasha could hear him asking Nia if she was good?

Sasha's voice raised two or three octaves as she asked, "Oh so you with your mannnn?" "Girl I'm on the way so be ready to pour the tea!" With that, Sasha ended the call.

Nia turned to Jihad and quickly caught him up on her plans to hang out with Sasha for the remainder of the afternoon before packing up and going home to her family.

"What's up?" Jihad questioned Nia after catching her looking at him kinda strange. "Huh", she replied, not realizing what he was referring to. "You're looking at me like you were thinking something." "Oh, um um", Nia stammered, not wanting to reveal her thoughts at the time. Nia had imagined, even daydreamed what "it" would feel like after being with Jihad for the first time but nothing, she had imagined could compare to what she actually felt. She was trying to be cool because she and Jihad had never actually discussed if she was a virgin or when the twosome would take their blossoming romance to the next level. Nia was not one to be short on words, but she was at a total loss for any word that could adequately describe how she felt even more connected with Jihad since making love with him last night.

Jihad pulled a wad of cash neatly wrapped in a thick rubber band out of his pocket and extended the hand full of money towards Nia. Before Nia could ask Jihad what it was for, he laughed at the widening of her eyes and said,

"Now, I know you're not about to ask me why I'm giving you this money."

That was exactly what Nia was about to do before Jihad made her seem silly for wondering such a thing. Overthinking was definitely a struggle for Nia so she reminded herself to get out of her own head and reached for the money as she kissed Jihad on the lips, saying, "You're the BEST boyfriend ever". Jihad returned the kiss and told Nia, "Call me when you get home later", playfully slapping her butt before walking out the suite.

Chapter Twenty-Three

Nia and Sasha had so much fun filling each other in on the excitement, challenges and adventures of life on their respective Historically Black Universities' campuses. There was no place on earth quite like the haven where a young mind could be educated, a soul could be inspired, potential manifested into promising futures and the camaraderie of new friendships turned to life-long family like the campuses of HBCUs all across the United States. The history of HBCUs

You could ask anyone that attended FAMU, Morehouse, Howard, Southern, Bethune, North Carolina A&T, Spelman, Tuskegee, Hampton, Florida Memorial, or any of the hundreds of HBCUs in the United States and the answer would be similar… "It was one of the best experiences of my life". HBCUs educated some of the most respected leaders in science, medicine, education, political science, and more. But in addition to a degree, you learn the importance of service and love of mankind, HBCU sporting events are magnified with the high energy of the proud perfectly choreographed members of the performing bands, and Greek sisterhoods and brotherhoods of sororities and fraternities that impact global change well beyond their days on the "yards" as the campuses were endearingly called.

The magnetic energy of the two young women must have permeated onto the other hotel guests because a waiter cheerfully delivered complimentary drinks to them from an anonymous resident. Sasha was more than ready to gulp hers down, but Nia was hesitant to drink it knowing she had to go home in a little while. She definitely didn't want Ms. Ali to think that she had gone to college and gotten buck wild by the social scenes that were no secret to college students. Besides, the two-piece bikinis may have mislead an observer to think the girls were at least twenty-one but Sasha's 19th birthday was approaching, and Nia wouldn't be 21 for a few more Decembers. Nia spoke up before Sasha could accept, "Please thank the sender but we'll have two virgin strawberry coladas with pineapple slices instead". Sasha pouted thinking, "Damn, Nia was still green as the grass on this beautifully landscaped lawn". Sasha loved her girl but geesh… she had just completed her first semester of college and she was ready to celebrate, especially if someone else was paying for it! Nia read the grimacing expression on Sasha's face and whispered,

"Girl, we don't know these people and we don't know who sent that drink but I'm not about to get set up for the *okey doke* over here on the beach cause the only faces that look like ours are the workers and that couple getting a massage in the private cabana". "Dang", Nia thought, that's all they needed, was to drink those drinks and then have someone ask them for ID. Sasha shrugged Nia off and said, "All I know is you owe me the drink that you just sent back to the bar Miss Goodie Two Shoes" and with that the girls burst into laughter and resumed talking about everything they hoped to do during their highly anticipated first collegiate summer break.

Nia pulled up to the moderate-sized yellow home with the white trimmed borders and felt a surge of excitement to see her mother and sister. Nia usually spoke to both of them at least a few times a week but she stilled missed them a lot. Meeting new people was fun and Nia enjoyed dormitory life as much as it could be enjoyed but there was just no place like home. Nia missed her favorite home cooked meals like barbeque lamb chops, cabbage with shredded carrots and yellow rice with buttered cornbread made from scratch. Her mouth watered thinking about the meals and desserts that she'd missed since leaving for Tallahassee.

Even though she really *really* wanted to surprise them both, she knew that could be potentially dangerous. Ms. Ali was a selfless mother and nurturing educator but growing up in the country had also taught her how to carry and shoot anything from a shotgun to a 380 caliber if and when necessary. It was nothing for a fox or snake to stray from the surrounding woods of her family's farmhouse in Georgia, so it went without saying that everybody knew how to handle a rifle and handgun by the age of six. Even though Nia had her house key, she thought it wise to ring the doorbell as she waited in anticipation.

When Jaz peeked out of her bedroom's window and saw Nia standing at the door, she began hollering and screaming so loudly until it alarmed Ms. Ali and they both almost collided as they dashed into the living room. Ms. Ali was just about to ask what all the fuss was about when she noticed Nia standing at the door.

Jaz opened the door and Momma Ali hugged both of her girls tightly as a barrage of chatter spilled out simultaneously. Ms. Ali wanted to know how did Nia get there? Jaz wanted to know if Nia had brought her anything? Nia wanted to know what was for dinner? They each tried to catch each other up on what had been going on since Nia left for school. All in all, everyone was fine. Jaz and Nia began to make plans to hang out for the holiday and Ms. Ali chimed in to remind the girls to plan to visit their father, aunts and uncles in between the mall, movies, and all the other things that were quickly building their itinerary.

Nia rolled her luggage inside and was slightly dismayed when she realized that Jaz had now taken over their once shared closet. Nia couldn't do anything but chuckle looking at the collection of fashion fancies her little sister had accumulated. Nia had always been the self- proclaimed fashionista of the two but apparently Jaz was no slouch. Nia eyed the array of textures ranging from faux fur to sequin fabrics, cropped graphic tees to patched denim trench coats. It looked like Nia would be living out of her bags for the next few weeks. She sat down on her bed and dialed Jihad. He didn't answer so she left a message. She realized that she really didn't get much sleep last night, so she laid her head on her pillow with her feet hanging off the bed. She didn't know all that this Christmas break had in store, but it was already off to an amazing start. There were no words to describe the feelings running through her body as she recalled making love to her best friend last night. Momma Ali had always strongly discouraged sex before marriage and Nia had heard enough of her friends share their regret of breaking their virginity with guys that ended up being players. In this moment, Nia only felt love and her connection to Jihad intensified as she drifted off to sleep.

Chapter Twenty-Four

Between all the fun and festivities of Christmas, Kwanzaa, and New Year's Eve, Nia wasn't sure if she was ready to leave the city lights of Miami to return to school in rural northern Florida. Tallahassee was a vibe unto itself, and she had finally begun to adjust to the nuances of collegiate life. Even with the preparation of high school guidance counselors, presentations of college recruiters, suggestions of college advisors and encouragement of supportive parents, navigating freshman year had come with a unique set of challenges. Campus security had been called to dormitory housing to settle heated catfights between feisty young ladies who were learning to live within new communities of people from all over the globe. Then there were the unyielding professors determined to keep their reputations of being the toughest classes to pass and male upperclassmen balancing testosterone and ego as they placed bets on who could smash the most 'fresh-meat' as the freshman girls were often referred to. Nia had managed to stay out of the path of the drama and completed first semester with a 3.69 GPA. She couldn't help but credit her mom's annoying reminders and her dreams of living life beyond the *Hill* with Jihad.

Nia felt her eyes welling up with tears when it was time to kiss Mama, Jaz, and Jihad goodbye but she had no choice once they approached Delta Airline's security gate at Miami International Airport. Nia usually was able to keep her emotions in check but at this moment she wasn't sure if she could stop the tears from falling. Attending college was an exciting adventure for which she was very grateful but unlike her friends that had called all throughout winter recess venting about ready to get away from the watchful eyes of their parent and their rules, Nia just couldn't relate. She had checked on her roommate, Shyanne, once or twice since arriving in Miami and she knew they'd have lots to talk about once they got back to school but there really was nothing like being surrounded by the people you love. Yeah, there were less parental restrictions away at college but Nia wasn't pressed about being home. Who could resist the delicious home cooked meals, aunts and uncles sliding neatly folded money in your hand as you departed, or the visits to the skating rink, movies, mall, bowling, and just hanging out with your favorite family and friends?

Both Nia and Jihad had avoided talking about her returning to school because they both didn't want to think about being separated during her spring semester of school. Even though Nia would have loved to spend more time with Jihad during her visit but he spent most of the time handling what he referred to as "*business*". Other than his responsibilities at the dry cleaners, Nia couldn't really see what all the ripping and running was about with him. She didn't pry because busy or not, he always checked on her and made sure she was good. She didn't have a chance to *want* for anything because he was always thinking ahead. She loved that about him. He wasn't just that way with her. If he cared about you, you couldn't help but know.

The distinct and exaggerated cough of the Delta Airline's representative interrupted Jihad's and Nia's long embrace. They hadn't realized that a line was forming behind them as others waited to enter the security checkpoint. Ms. Ali had patiently waited a few feet away, but her patience was wearing thin as she thought to herself, "Why were these two behaving so dramatically as if Nia wouldn't be back in Miami within the next four months?" Jihad stepped back from Nia, then leaned in and whispered something in her ear. Nia giggled then joined the moving line of travelers as they began disrobing their jackets, jewelry and shoes. Ms. Ali gave Jihad the side eye as she thought, "I don't know what y'all whispering and giggling about but all I know is Nia betta not come back from FAMU carrying nothing besides her degree." Jaz laughed aloud as she peeped Ms. Ali giving Jihad one questionable look. Jihad led the remaining Ali women to the Porsche SUV that he borrowed from his Uncle Bo so that they could all accompany Nia to the airport and fit the two bags she brought with her plus the two new large suitcases she managed to fill during her stay. Jihad grew up in a home with his mother and twin sisters so women spending hours on end in a mall didn't surprise him, but he never understood why it took them all day to find what they wanted from the mall. He and most of the guys in his hood, always knew exactly what he was going to the mall for, what store had it, and on what end of the mall he needed to park in order to get in and out quickly. His mind drifted to random thoughts of what the coming days would bring as he felt Nia's absence already.

Nia was seated in row four, seat A; always a window seat for her. Her seat was reclined as she lay back with her eyes closed. Nia's thoughts drifted to her mental to-do-list. First and foremost, she needed to meet with her college advisor; she wanted to make sure she understood the timeline of her course requirements so she could stay on track for graduation. Nia knew her decision to go to FAMU was the right choice, but she was already missing her family and her boyfriend so much. She just wanted to get back to Tally and back to the books. The sooner she got started, the closer she'd be to her Bachelor of Science degree in journalism. She had every reason to work hard now so she'd be able to manifest a bright and beautiful future.

A polite yet stern voice sounded over the PA. "Ladies and gentlemen, please prepare for landing. Return your seats to the upright position fasten your seatbelts and ensure all table trays are secured. We are descending into the Tallahassee Airport and the current temperature is 54 degrees. It has been our pleasure to serve you and we look forward to your next flight with Delta Airlines."

The airline cabin began to fill with chatter as the flight attendant who was standing at the front of the aircraft giving landing instructions awakened sleeping passengers. Many on board clapped and cheered welcoming the dissension of the Boeing 747 aircraft as the pilot guided it towards the runway.

Nia's eyes were fixated on the landmass of trees and city streets below. She loved to travel and even though Tallahassee was small compared to Miami, being thirty thousand feet in the air, amongst the majestic clouds, always made her feel a sense of peace. Nia looked up and noticed that the sky was clear and beautiful hues of baby blue as they met the runway. Nia hadn't arranged a ride to the dorm, so she knew she'd have to take an expensive cab or Super Shuttle if they had any space for non- confirmed riders. The plane hit the ground with a hard thump and Nia grabbed the seat in front of her to avoid hitting her head on the headrest. She was so glad she was seated near the front; she hated waiting for everyone that had to retrieve all of their carry-on bags from the overhead bins. She grabbed her Louis Vuitton monogramed backpack from underneath the seat in front of her, pulled her mirrored Ray-Ban aviator sunglasses out and put them on top of her head before deplaning. All she could think was, "here I go, back to the future".

Chapter Twenty-Five

*I*t was relatively easy to get back into the daily routine of attending classes, labs, study groups, and one-to-one chats during professors' office hours. Nia was excited to have successfully completed almost two years of her undergraduate journey. The seasons of winters, springs, summers, and falls continued to pass on the universe's divine calendar. Even though Nia was a bonafide South Florida sunshine girl, she really enjoyed living through all of the seasons. Nothing would ever compare to the feeling of the sun's warmth sinking into her pecan tan hued skin or strolling down the ocean's shore as warm sand slipped between perfectly polished hot pink pedicured toes. Yet, Nia still welcomed the cool breeze of the fall in Tallahassee and the brisk, chill air that allowed her to wear graphic sweatshirts, sweaters and peacoats in an array of fabrics ranging from soft cashmere to the heavier wool blends.

One of the down sides of living in the dorm had to share restroom and shower facilities with others who lived on the same floor. Nia had expressed her concerns with resident assistant, her mom, and Jihad but they all basically said the same thing: "You have the option of moving off campus". Freshman students were required to live on campus, but once

Nia became a sophomore, she had no one to blame but herself. The more she thought about it, she considered her homegirl's offer to become roommates at a nice rental townhome about 2.5 miles from campus.

Nia weighed the pros and cons; it was just convenient to live on campus. Sure there were a lot of perks to living off campus, like no housing restrictions and the freedom to create your own living space to your liking. A lot of people enjoyed hanging out at card parties, letting loose on the weekends at house parties and the privacy of having their boyfriend or girlfriend stay over without having to compromise with a roommate or watch out for the RAs. Nia really didn't have to think about the whole boyfriend thing because Jihad was in Miami. When he did visit, he always got a suite for them at one of the boutique hotels in Tally. Convenience had won out in the past year and a half, but Nia could feel herself growing beyond the mental and physical space of dorms. Between Ms. Ali and scholarships, Nia, unlike many of her peers, never had taken a student loan to finance her education. But moving off campus would present another level of financial responsibility and Nia just wanted to seriously consider how that may impact her as far as possibly getting a part-time job or staying on track for graduation. Her dad was always willing to send money for books or emergency spending cash, but Nia didn't want to make any decisions that would add more financial weight on her mother. Ms. Ali worked two jobs to provide for her family and it was a sacrifice that was never far from Nia's mind.

She knew the one person that would give her solid advice in an honest yet compassionate way. Nia picked her phone up and called her Grandma Lillie. After a several rings, a voice as raspy as wind rustling through autumn leaves answered, "Hello".

"Heyyyyy Grandma, how ya doing?" Nia could feel Grandma Lillie smiling through the phone as she answered, "Well, well what a welcome surprise! I wasn't doing much of nothing rat nie" in her sweet southern drawl. "I done been out early dis morning feedin dem chicken and cleaning the coup. One of da hawgs got out da pin so I had to send one o Richard's boys out dere to brang em back. I gotta good crop of greens so me and Lizzie gon pick em a lil later. Enuf about me, how you doing?" she asked. "How dem folks in Tall-ee-has-ee been treating my favorite gurl? Nia chuckled to herself because she had no doubt that Grandma Lillie loved her beyond infinity, but she also felt that Grandma Lillie probably called each of her grandchildren *favorite* when speaking with them. It was just her way. Whether you were family, a friend, or a complete stranger, you could always depend on Grandma Lillie to have a good meal on the table, food stored in preserve jars, deep freezers, or ready to be plucked right from her garden of field peas, lima beans, collard greens, turnip greens, tomatoes and so many other home-grown vegetables. But more importantly, Grandma's house was like a temple of loving wisdom. As the daughter of sharecroppers, Grandma Lillie had lived through many of the injustices documented in Nia's humanities and history books, but her strong faith had freed her from bitterness which she shared is a foundation for love and wisdom. Summer visits to the country was still one of Nia's favorite past times. The country's air just expanded your lungs differently. Inhaling nature's perfumes of peach and pear trees, blooming pink trumpet plants, or the round and juicy scuppernongs whose vines hugged the makeshift wire fence that helped keep the threats of wild critters at bay, invigorated the body and stimulated the mind.

"Grandma?", Nia said as she broke away from her childhood memories.

"Yes, honey…", Grandma Lillie replied. "I'm almost halfway through my four years of college and right now, I'm still living on campus, but I'm getting frustrated with the living arrangements." Nia shared.

"Frustrated about what? How dey treatin' you down there? Grandma asked.

"Oh, it's not that. For the most part, everyone is pretty friendly, and the professors are very helpful. It' just that in the dorms where I live, I only have to share a bedroom with one other girl but everyone on the same hallway shares the same restroom and showers."

"Wellllll, grandma replied, I imagine many sacrifices are made to get from one level to another in life. I ain't never been to no college; didn't even make it to high school for having to help raise my momma's youngins and helping farm the crops but I know a lot about sacrifice. What you gotta consider is, is your frustration stealing your joy and peace and if the answer is yes, you got to decide if you're willing to do what it takes to eliminate your frustration and get your joy back. See either way you slice it, you gon make sacrifices in life if you plan to accomplish anything worthwhile. But don't let nothing or nobody steal your joy, even in the midst of your dilemma. Figure out what it's costing you to stay in that dorm and factor in your frustration too, then figure out what will it cost you to get somewea wea you can study and live wit a lil mo privacy. If you willing to get a lil job or see if you qualify for other scholarships, you'll be all right. Nia you're a smart cookie; I ain't neva worried about you gettin lost in this ole world. If you get a job, you'll sacrifice some of yo free time, but you'll have privacy. If you stay in the dorm, you'll have more free time but less privacy. Dem yo two options. Either way it goes, never let something temporary frustrate you to the point that you stop being productive. Whether you share a restroom or not, you learn all dat you can and then you make sho to teach it to someone else."

Grandma Lillie didn't speak the Queen's English, but she was a queen in her own right. She was the family's matriarch filled with her own hidden pains that she kept to herself and selflessly shared her happiness with anyone she came into contact with. Nia knew that her grandmother's advice would help her clear her thoughts and decide what her next steps would be. Nia was sure that she had interrupted something grandma was doing because she hardly ever sat still but she also knew that her Grandma Lillie was never too busy to chat with her. Nia made a mental note to visit her one weekend soon just to give her a big hug and kiss.

"Thanks for everything grandma," Nia said and to which grandma replied, "No thanks needed at all baby. Just stay focused on reaching your goals and learn all that you can. Then, don't forget to share what you're learning with others along your way." Nia could hear the movement of her getting up from the wooden dining table, which had become the meeting center for family matters. Grandma would pull out a fresh baked cake or pie, cut a few slices and listen intently without interrupting whoever was seeking some heartfelt advice. Nia thought it funny, that grandma would sit there even though she was four hours away in her dorm room. But she knew that the table was more than a place to eat and talk, it represented generations of family members' praying, eating, and pushing through whatever trouble or triumph the day may have brought.

Nia said, "I love you Grandma, I'll keep you posted".

Grandma Lillie smiled to herself and told Nia, "Everything is going to be okay. Pray about everything and worry about nothing. Now I gotta get outside and see what's running my chickens"

Nia laughed at the last part of her comment and blew a kiss through the phone before placing it on the receiver.

Chapter Twenty-Six

Nia was studying for her Psychology exam when the phone rang. She answered and was pleased to hear Jihad on the other line.

"What's up, you busy, Jihad asked?"

Nia *was* busy but she welcomed the brain break to talk with her boo.

"I was but, I'm good, how are you?"

Jihad paused like he wasn't sure if he should offer to just call back, but Nia interrupted his thoughts, "What's going on? I'm good".

"Well, I've got some news; I hope you like it."

"Okay, what's the news that you hope I like?" Nia asked with a half smirk. She didn't know what Jihad was up to, but he seemed reluctant to just spit it out.

Jihad said, "I'm moving to Tallahassee". The words flowed out his mouth sounding more like a declaration than an intention or plan. Nia heard what Jihad said but yet the phone line went silent.

"Nia, did you hear me?"

Nia couldn't believe her ears and she really wanted to, so she said, "Say that again".

"I said, I'm moving to Tally" Jihad repeated.

Nia's heart began to race as she tried to wrap her mind around the news Jihad had just shared. She was ecstatic and a bit confused as to how he had come to this major decision. His family and family business had always been the center of every decision he made so Nia couldn't help but wonder what was going on in Miami?

Nia remembered planning a surprise mini-vacation for the two of them to visit the Disney World theme park in Orlando, FL a few weeks before she left for her freshman year of college and being extremely disappointed by his refusal to go. Jihad had said that he was sorry, but he couldn't just drop his responsibilities at the cleaners and go on a surprise trip. It had broken Nia's heart, but she didn't let him know it. She shrugged it off and said, "Maybe another time" as she blinked back tears. She had put so much thought and detail into planning that trip, even down to their itinerary of the popular restaurants, luxurious spas, and ideal locations for vacation photo shoots. It was that day that Nia realized and accepted the hold Jihad's family had on him; the sense of responsibility he felt was like an anchor tied to the heart of everything he did. Nia loved Jihad's sense of love and loyalty. It was something she had come to respect and admire. It hadn't always been easy for Jihad to balance his family's business obligations and their relationship, but he made it clear that she was an important part of his life and future. In return, her love for him helped her to accept that his life wasn't one that he'd chosen but it was the hand he had been dealt. If she loved him and she did indeed love him, it was the hand they both would have to play. They shared an unspoken understanding. Nia could see the internal conflict that Jihad struggled with concerning things he'd never verbally shared with her. She just wanted to be his soft place in the world, away from the business, the streets, and the quiet chaos in which he navigated.

Nia finally said, "yes, I heard you and of course I'm so happy to hear that you're moving to Tally but how did this all come about?"

Jihad took a deep breath and said, "It's a long story but I've already applied to TCC and gotten accepted, so I'll begin next semester. I'll be up there in two weeks to look for a place and I really want you to move with me in our own place"

Nia wanted to scream, "From your mouth to God's ears" but instead she quickly jumped off her bed and began jumping up and down. After about twenty seconds of her private celebration, she calmly replied, "Yes and yes to everything you just said! I love you, Jihad!" Nia could feel Jihad exhale as if he ever thought for a second that she would decline his offer.

Jihad said, "I'll let you know when I work out my travel details but start looking in the classified and apartment guides for some places you wanna check out when I get there."

"Okay", Nia replied, and they agreed to talk later about their plans.

Nia fell back on to the mountain of decorative pillows on her bed and began to daydream of how perfect everything was going. She had been applying for jobs, grants, and scholarships in hopes of earning more money to assist in her move off campus. She hadn't even discussed it with Jihad and yet the stars were aligning so that she wouldn't spend her junior year of college on campus in a cramped dormitory room. She'd miss the camaraderie of the girl talk, live-in study partners, and on-campus social life but it was time to take the next step of independence. She knew Ms. Ali would disapprove of Nia and Jihad living together without being married so she'd have to think about how to break the news to her. For the most part, she'd always tried to respect her mother's ideals but at some point, everybody has to live their own life. Nia twist and turned until she lay comfortably on her side and dozed off happily at the anticipation of new beginnings.

Chapter Twenty-Seven

Psychological statistics had proven to be the absolute hardest class in Nia's course load to date. Research had never been a problem for Nia; she actually enjoyed the process of weaving information together in a way that was informative, interesting, and engaging. But numbers had never been her thing or at least that's the story she had replayed in her own mind since leaving Mr. Johnson's sixth grade class. Mr. Johnson was the last person to help Nia make sense of numerical functions and applications. So, when Professor Blackshear explained that the course would involve the relationship of psychological techniques and principles to statistical data, Nia felt doomed from the jump.

Nia had attended every study group, met with Professor Blackshear for countless office conferences and yet she still fell short of passing the class. She was almost in tears when he returned the students' final exams and she saw the large 67% marked in bright red ink at the top. Professor Blackshear had already told Nia that she would have to earn at least a 70% to pass the class. Her research paper had pulled her grade up, but it was her test and quiz scores that kept impeding her success. She was overtaken with despair. Four months, one hundred twenty days, two thousand eight hundred and eighty hours of psychological statistics on her brain had drained her mentally and emotionally and she didn't think she could go through it again. It felt hopeless. Even when she felt like she was beginning to understand, she would hold her breath when the professor returned the papers, silently praying that she had gotten a passing grade. She had managed to perform well on a few tests but not consistently enough to pull off at least a C in the class. Nia was physically 5 feet 6 and ½ inches but today she felt two feet tall. She had earned As and Bs in her other classes, but she had still failed to pull it off in the psyche class. Oh well, Nia thought, I better schedule an appointment with my advisor to see if it the class will be offered during summer? She didn't blame Professor Blackshear even though she felt like he could've given her a little grace concerning the three points. She wasn't hopeful that another four months of the same curriculum, with the same professor was going to fare any better. So, Nia made a mental note to ask two important questions when she spoke with her advisor;

1. if the class was offered during summer, 2. if there was another professor teaching it, and if neither of the other two options were possible, could she take it at another school's campus? Professor Blackshear was engaging, humorous and knowledgeable but Nia needed a miracle worker to earn a passing grade in his class. There was nothing she could do about the D she'd earned in his class at this moment, so she decided to go to the mall for a little retail therapy. A nice pair of stilettos or new handbag was sure to lift her spirits.

Nia heard her phone ringing as she rushed to unlock her dorm room door. She dropped her shopping bags on to her bed and nearly knocked everything on her desk to the floor as she dashed to pick it up.

"Hello, hello?" Nia panted as she tried to catch her breath. "Hello?" she repeated but the only sound Nia heard on the other line was a dial tone. She placed the phone down on the hook and sat down as she tried to resume her normal breathing. She wondered who was calling her midday, but she didn't think on it too long. Nia's roommate entered shortly after and burst into laughter at the mess Nia was currently sitting comfortably in the middle of. An array of outfits that she needed to hang up, shopping bags from her shopping day, the three handbags that she'd chosen not to wear today, and her backpack were all scattered atop her twin sized bed.

Nia's day had been as colorful as the rainbow; yellow as she awoke hoping to have passed Professor Blackshear's class; purple as she felt the brewing red of anger and the blue of sadness upon receiving her final; the relaxing vibrations of green as she strolled through the mall trying to release the anxiety of her day, and now gray as she sat solemnly on her bed in the midst of all the reminders that she needed to get up and get it together. Just as Nia's feet hit the floor, her phone rang but this time she calmly reached for it, saying "Hello" in a monotone drenched in fatigue.

"Hey babe, Jihad replied, and Nia's eyes lit up and the corners of her mouth turned up in joy. Jihad had impeccable timing and Nia felt the warmth of the pot of gold to her rainbow.

Chapter Twenty-Eight

Jihad and Nia had found and settled into a nice two-bedroom villa centrally located between the Tallahassee Community College and FAMU campuses. Nia was excited to decorate and make their first home together cute and comfortable. Jihad didn't concern himself with the details of bath décor or living room accent pillows, but he didn't complain as he drove Nia from store to store. He never would've imagined that a city as quaint as Tally had this many stores for home design. At one point, he had told Nia that he'd sit it out in the car. Nia felt like she was beginning to push her luck, so she made their visit to Steinmart her last store for today. Nia had appreciated Jihad's willingness to go along with her home shopping spree even though she knew it was probably because he really didn't have anything else to do and even if this wasn't his idea of a favorite pastime, she could tell he was happy about this new chapter they were embarking upon also.

Jihad was laid back on the soft white Natuzzi leather sectional searching for a good Sunday football game on the 54-inch Sony floor model television. The only two must-haves Jihad insisted on was the television and a subdivision that had a basketball court. He had to forego his third preference, which was a residence with a security gate, but guard gated subdivisions weren't as common in Tally as they were in Miami, which was understandable considering the vast difference in crime rates between the two Florida cities.

Nia had meticulously decorated the master bathroom with ivory and gold bath towels that were hung upside down and tied with black tassel cords. She then rolled and placed black, ivory and gold jacquard printed towels within the upside-down bath décor arrangement. She had placed a tall black lacquer vase in the corner of the countertop and inserted a tall, vibrant green bamboo plant. The glass shower doors made the bathroom appear larger than it was and the large, matte silver, rectangular-shaped mirror was a classy statement piece to complete the look. Nia stood back and admired her work. She remembered childhood days when Ms. Ali would visit new construction model homes and stroll through admiring the beautiful and unique rooms of décor. Nia had fallen in love with how home decorators would mix and match expensive and thrift home accessories to each room to display unique living spaces for prospective buyers. Jihad hadn't given Nia a budget, but it was more of a hobby to her. She'd spend hours searching high-end consignment and thrift shops for just the perfect piece for their home. After hours of sanding and painting the wooden rectangular mirror that she found in Goodwill, the silver mirror accented with faux distressed black cracks, hung on the wall horizontally adding the illusion of more space. As a personal housewarming gift, Nia ordered matching white terrycloth robes with their monogrammed initials in black. Jihad hadn't seen them yet;

Nia wanted to hang them on the back of the door but had forgotten to buy the decorative hooks.

Nia was almost finished making the bed and sighed when she glanced towards the corner of the room and winced at a pile of pillows suitable for at least three beds. Nia didn't know where her obsession for lots of bed pillows came from but somewhere along the way it had gotten out of hand. She'd purchased square, round, sham, European, and decorative pillows and pillowcases to compliment the Tiffany blue comforter set from Steinmart. Before she could begin arranging the pillows, Jihad wrapped his arms around her from the back and turned her around to face him. He had been standing in the door for a few minutes observing her and smiled to himself how intentional she was about making everything perfect for their new home. He loved Nia and he knew that she loved him too.

"Are you hungry?", he asked.

"A little but I don't know what I want."

"Well, I know exactly what I have an appetite for", Jihad, said as he pulled her down onto him in the center of the king size, four- poster bed.

"Jihaaddd" Nia squealed playfully as if he was interrupting something that couldn't be resumed later. "You know I need to finish this."

"I know baby" he replied as he slowly created a path of wet kisses from her face, lips, and neck down to her soft rounded breast.

Jihad had applied the pressure of his body's weight to glide Nia onto the bed. Even if she had been strong enough to resist, she couldn't imagine why she would. His caramel hued skin felt so warm, his arms enveloping her with his strength. She felt the throbbing sensation of her inner womanhood and let out the softest sound of pleasure as his hands caressed her body. Nia wrapped her arms around Jihad's back and stroked his toned frame from his shoulders to beneath his waist. It didn't take long for their bodies to move in unison, becoming one passionate force of energy. Beads of sweat trickled down their skin. Nia could feel Jihad's heartbeat increasing in speed and he felt the intensity of her pulsating muscles contracting on his manhood; tightening her core around him and releasing in perfectly random increments. Nia felt light and free as she wrapped her leg around Jihad's back and applied just enough pressure to reposition herself so that she was now on top of him. Nia and Jihad had shared some pretty amazing intimate moments whether under the stars of Miami's beaches, on a private chartered yacht during their vacation in the Bahamas or long car rides to nowhere just vibing with the sunroof opened as they shared their dreams. The intensity of their lovemaking had come in waves as they'd grown closer but right here in this moment, they had evolved from making love to sharing love. How was it that the more one gave, the love returned to them intensified, magnified, and greater than it had been given? Their souls translated a language only understood between them and it was difficult to completely feel each other because it was like trying to feel a part of yourself from the inside. The freshly made bed sheets were now damp from the perspiration on their wet bodies.

Chapter Twenty-Nine

Jihad was naturally book smart but not necessarily studious. The responsibilities of his family's business had been a considerable distraction from his attention to school. He'd always tested well and achieved high marks when he applied himself, but hustling was in his DNA. He'd lost too many childhood associates to the streets so he learned firsthand that the streets didn't love anybody, and lack of focus could be a lethal flaw. He couldn't commit to both, so the money won.

Jihad was a young man of few words and a deep thinker. A quiet observer, he preferred leaning in to what people chose not to say. He had been exposed to the hood's blueprint of achieving wealth and held himself to the code of death before dishonor. Jihad carried a lot of weight on his shoulders, and it wasn't until after high school that he started reevaluating where the path he was on would lead. As the eldest and only son, he had inherited this life of man-child responsibilities and never questioned himself or his parents because to be honest, he'd earned more money than the average adult that worked a 9-5 and that was just during his high school years.

Months before Jihad moved to Tally, he sat in the back of the United States Federal Courthouse courtroom holding his breath with his face pressed into the palms of his hands as the judge handed down a 30-year sentence on his partner and brother. The look of defeat in Demond's eyes as he glanced back at his girl, his son, daughter, and parents, was the catalyst for Jihad's change of heart. It wasn't the first time someone from around his way was arrested or sent to prison, but Demond was the older brother Jihad never had. Sure, he had his dad and uncles but with Demond being just a few years older than Jihad, they had been as close as blood brothers. He'd given him game on so many things like avoiding the girls that were pretty to look at but poison to touch. Charismatic and enticing, these young hood stars had learned their own ways to navigate the jungle and they knew how to use their beauty, booty, and brains to get what they wanted. Some of them jumped off the porch as young girls and had soaked up the ways of the older women around them. Whether it was finessing a man out of his money for their time or walking through the mall running scams for the latest fashion, they were just as much of hustlers as their male counterparts.

The bond that Demond and Jihad shared had been formed since their childhood of riding bikes, playing basketball on the park's courts, skipping school for one reason or another to climbing out of the trenches in the hood. When Jihad got the call from Demond's kids' mom, he knew it couldn't be good. A call from a man's mother or woman was usually a sign of trouble or death where they were from. Jihad was relieved it was the latter but sitting in this courtroom, his heart sank as he saw his homeboy turn and glance at his family knowing that despite his sacrifices and efforts, his current situation was out of his hands. Demond had already spent 200k on his legal team and despite the sentence, at least he'd beat the possibility of life without the parole. He could only imagine how much the appeal was gonna cost him, but he knew Jihad would hold his family down while he sat through the process.

Betrayal was worse than death and it cut Demond deep to have to sit and watch one of his closest homies testify against him. Demond had never intricately involved Bam Bam in his hustle, but he was one of the little homies that just like being around. He was more of a runner for food, girls, or whatever entertainment Demond and his crew were feeling for the night. He kept Demond informed on the tedious but significant details about things going on off his immediate radar.

Bam Bam's mom worked two jobs to keep a roof over their heads, so Demond was more of a father figure and someone to look out for him while his mom was at work. The feds played hardball and they had been investigating a large multi-state criminal operation for two years, which had helped them link everyone between the boss and the weakest link. They pulled up on Bam Bam one night while he was running an errand for Demond. They had a stack of photos of the hood's who's who, implicating Bam Bam in Demond's daily business operations. Bam Bam wasn't chasing money or a dream, he just liked the way the girls around the way flashed their pearly whites at him when he was spotted driving one of Demond's luxury cars around. A couple of them had even given up the goodies hoping to finesse their way to the real breadwinners in the circle. He had never been a part of any of Demond's money moves but had heard and seen just enough to make him credible to a federal jury.

Jihad and Demond had an unspoken childhood pact. Both, determined to get out of the hood and live lives that defied the odds. From real estate to the stock market, they figured once they stacked enough money, they would create other legitimate opportunities for their families and youngsters facing similar adversities that they'd faced. For the most part, they'd swam amongst sharks without being devoured. They'd caught a few petty charges of possession of marijuana or cocaine with intent to sale but were never convicted. The cops would charge you for being in the car of a homeboy who had a personal stash on him or for standing within a group when they pulled up if someone was holding. Hell, sometimes a dirty cop would put the dope in your pocket. That was their version of the war on drugs.

Demond had moved to a condo in Miami Lakes, a step up from the inner city where he'd grown up. He'd made life comfortable for his girlfriend and children and was working on a master plan to invest in commercial real estate. One of his Cuban homies had an uncle with a savvy real estate group and Demond knew his next business transaction would add enough zeroes to his bank account to give him a seat at the corporate table. He worked his way up from detailing cars at a local, popular spot to eventually buying it from the older guy who'd grown weary with how it had become a hangout for a lot of younger people. He loved the business, but he wasn't up for the large crowds. His dismay was Demond's opportunity to put his savings to good use. Once he'd paid his last installment on the deal, he added a small menu and upgraded the customer waiting area. He leveraged the crowd's desire to convene into more money for the business. Demond was sharp and continued to go after his dreams by promoting two nights a week at a local club. He enjoyed the material trappings that money bought but he wanted more than money, would go against all odds to give his children a better start than he had.

Jihad sat in silence as the federal bailiff approached Demond and motioned for him to stand as he was taken into custody. Demond would have bet nearly everything he had on the loyalty of the team of partners that he'd formed business and personal relationships with over the years. He never imagined a non-factor like Bam Bam would jam him like this. He'd slipped and now it was costing him his family and his freedom.

Jihad walked over to Demond's family and wrapped his arm around his mother. He tried to console them but how when he felt their pain? He ushered them out of the courtroom as they wiped their tears away. When they reached the parking garage, Jihad offered to take them all out for a bite to eat but they declined. They didn't have an appetite and they wanted to be home just in case Demond called. They embraced and Jihad ensured them that he'd stop by later to check on them for which they were grateful.

As Jihad looked in his rear-view mirror to back out of his parking space, he knew that he had to choose a different path. It broke his heart to watch one of his closest friends be walked in the opposite direction of his family and it was a feeling he never wanted to know for himself.

Chapter Thirty

Many of the young people that went off to college, had been preparing and dreaming about the experience since beginning high school, if not longer. However, the path Jihad was now embarking was a detour from a life he thought he was destined to live. During high school, he'd observed various groups of people move with excitement when they engaged in learning and career-oriented activities. The JROTC students were uniformed, disciplined, and cohesive; they moved as one unit when following the commands of their leader. Jihad knew that joining the military wasn't his path, but he respected the principle of teamwork that the military embodied. The Future Business Leaders of America students eagerly engaged in local and state speaking and critical thinking competitions in pursuit of scholarship awards, job opportunities, and internships in industries of interest. Some of the smartest kids in the school were in multiple club organizations and were still able to maintain high grades. All of this was going on around Jihad and yet he hadn't seriously considered anything other than managing his family's growing businesses. When Bam Bam flipped on Demond, Jihad was forced to take a closer look at his own future and make some impromptu choices.

Jihad wrestled with how to share his decision to move to Tallahassee and study Business Administration at the local community college with his immediate family. His parents had come to rely on his abilities and willingness to handle the day-to-day operations of the cleaners and monitor other family investments around town. Jihad had been groomed to take over a dream that he hadn't chose but had rather inherited. As a youngster, that level of responsibility was flattering but as a young man, it was weighing heavily upon him. Growing up in the inner city, money or the lack of money was the topic of most people's discussions and focus. The goal for the average person was to get money and if they were dreamers, getting out of the hood was a bonus.

Jihad was grateful that his mother was a legend in her own right when it came to making something out of nothing. She had taken a small financial opportunity and finessed it into her own family empire. Years before the twins were born, Queen, as she was affectionately known, was struggling to raise Jihad alone. Her high school sweetheart, Johnny, had taken a job as a long-distance truck driver to earn more money. For the few years, he'd sent weekly checks to help support Jihad but over time, the money and calls became less frequent. Whenever he came to town, he'd pick Jihad up and take him to the basketball court, beach, or an inside amusement spot and let him run, play, and laugh until he was exhausted.

One day, Queen who had been lying awake in bed, jumped up, showered, and got dressed. She didn't have a destination in mind, but she felt led to take the bus that drove to Miami Beach. Most blacks that were on the bus going there either worked in restaurants or cleaned the beautiful mansions and hotels along the ocean shore. Queen had worked odd jobs here and there to support her and Jihad, but she was never satisfied with the low wages or treatment by the supervisors. As she sat by the window, she stared at the beautiful homes along the bus route. Some of them seemed to take up a city block. Foreign design cars lined the pristine driveways and every so often she would catch a glimpse of a family or two leisurely enjoying their lifestyles.

Queen's mind had drifted as she imagined a life like the ones she saw from a distance. She was startled when the bus driver called out to her loudly,

"Ma'am, ma'am this is the last stop on this route." Queen eyes blinked repeatedly as if she was trying to gain her focus as she gathered her tan distressed leather handbag and exited the bus.

As soon as her feet hit the pavement, she was drawn to the sounds of the waves crashing upon the shore. She waited for the oncoming traffic to yield and when she reached the sand, she slid her sandals off and dug her toes into the warm sand before heading towards the beach. Children were throwing frisbees and flying kites and laughter could be heard as they ran and played with their friends. Queen sat a few feet from the water and meditated on how she could change the course of her life. Without warning a little blonde-haired girl ran up to her and lightly touched Queen's hair. Startled, Queen looked around to see whom the little girl was with. A young woman with long blonde hair ran up to Queen speaking another language and making gestures of an apology. All the while the toddler seemed enamored with Queen's braided hairstyle. Within minutes an older gentleman approached and spoke to the young woman in the unknown language. He then, chuckled and asked Queen in English if she knew where his daughter and granddaughter could get their hair braided like hers? Apparently, they were visiting from Italy and were fascinated with the braided hairstyle. Queen was surprised and flattered and offered to braid their hair herself. She thought to herself, "It's not like I'm out here doing anything; I can make this money." The gentleman seemed pleased that he could oblige them during their vacation and gave a teenage boy a crisp $20 bill to bring three beach chairs to their location.

Queen stood as they both waited patiently as the other's hair was braided. The little girl got two braids because she wasn't going to sit for much more than that, but her mother received ten braids styled going back and she absolutely loved them both. She didn't speak English according to her father but when Queen handed her the compact mirror from her purse, the wide smile on her face told Queen all she needed to know. Queen welcomed the pleasant disruption of her thoughts and hadn't considered the payment for her labor. Her eyes widened as the gentleman reached inside his pocket and pulled out a monogrammed money clip with a wad of crisp $100 bills. He handed Queen a single bill with Benjamin Franklin's face on it and now Queen was the one with a big smile on her face. The gentleman thanked her again as he escorted the bubbly twosome towards the other end of the beach. Queen stood almost in disbelief at how she had made $100 in less than 45 minutes. The sun was beginning to set, and Queen observed all the families along the beach who traveled from near and far to vacation here and an idea popped into her head.

During the bus ride home, she scribbled notes and strategies about her new business ideas on a napkin that she'd had in her purse. Beach Babes and Braids were created from a chance encounter with a little girl and her mother who didn't speak English but had simply admired her hair. Her new entrepreneurial journey would prove exciting and exhausting, but it created viable profits for Queen as the owner and competitive wages for the young women that she employed along the beach shore to accommodate tourists from all over the world with beautiful braid designs. Queen had earned her right to sit on the throne of her family businesses and Jihad had nothing but the utmost respect and love for his mom and her accomplishments. The tug pulling in Jihad's chest made it less easy to tell her that he would be leaving to go to Tallahassee for school. When he walked in the kitchen, Queen was standing at the counter chopping vegetables to prepare dinner. "Ma? Jihad called out to her. "Huh," Queen replied as she continued what she was doing.

'I'm moving to Tallahassee in a couple of weeks for school." "School" Queen repeated in a tone that seemed like an inquiry and statement simultaneously.

"Yea, I already applied and got accepted to study business administration."

Queen turned around to face Jihad and asked, "Why would you need to study business when you been handling business since middle school? Are you sure this is about school or is this about that girl?"

Jihad knew this conversation wouldn't be easy, but he had hoped it wouldn't turn into an argument either. His mind was made up, but he hoped his mother would give her well wishes for him to consider and pursue his own goals.

"Nah, this ain't about Nia. Yea she's in school up there and we're good but she had nothing to do with my decision to go to school. It's just a lot going on down here and I figured now would be a good time as any to create my own path."

"Your own path, huh?" Queen asked. "Suit yourself." With that, Queen turned around and continued preparing dinner. Jihad could see the disappointment in her eyes. He felt that she saw his choice as more of a decision to leave everything she'd worked so hard as opposed to an internal pulling to discover his own way. It wasn't an easy decision for him either but when was there ever a time that becoming your own man was easy?

Chapter Thirty-One

Jihad received his first semester schedule in the mail and chuckled to himself at the sight of his name and information at the top of the page; student name, ID number, Classification. Jihad was a college freshman. Even a year ago, no one could've told him he'd be here; in college. He wasn't sure if he was up for the challenge but as he walked down the corridor towards his first class, he knew he'd give it his best shot and see where this school thing led him.

College was so different from high school. After Professor Weaver called all of the students' names and had everyone to check their schedules to ensure they were in the correct class, the remainder of the class was less traditional than what Jihad expected. The professor explained that he would use random selection to assign each person to a group until he learned more about them personally. The cohorts would collaborate and participate in competitions during debates and Socratic Seminar discussions. Jihad had heard just enough to consider dropping this class and adding a different one. He was not fond of public speaking, especially in front of a group of people he didn't know or care to know. As he perused the students in the class, he couldn't imagine what they would have in common that would be discussion worthy. Professor

Weaver intuitively sensed the reluctance in his students' eyes and body language and asked everyone to stand to their feet as he began to pass out colored index cards. Students were asked to join other students with the same color index card as they were given. Jihad joined a group of four other students and wasn't surprised that he was the only African American male in the class. Most of the guys he knew that went to college attended Division 1A or HBCUs on athletic scholarships. Some earned scholarships in both as academic scholars. Jihad actually could've attended a community college in Miami but that would have defeated the purpose in figuring some things out in his own space and on his own time.

The semesters continued to roll by, and Nia was so glad that Jihad had decided to come to Tallahassee and attend college. She could see him evolving beyond the comfort zone of everything that had become second nature to him growing up in the inner city of Miami. They would share discussions about things they learned in their respective classes, and he seemed to be enjoying the peace of the distinct differences from the hustle and bustle of home. Jihad was still reserved; untrusting of strangers and even some that he knew well but he began to embrace that his world was opening up like a flower that blooms in springtime.

Nia was washing the dishes from the couple's early dinner when she heard Jihad's beeper about to buzz right off the countertop. "Jiiiihhhaaaadddd", she yelled out to him, but he didn't answer. A few moments later the beeper began buzzing back-to-back. Apparently, whoever was trying to reach him didn't plan to wait long for a reply.

"Jihad, your beeper is about to blow up", Nia hollered out. Still, he didn't respond. Reaching for a dishtowel, Nia dried her hands and left the kitchen with Jihad's beeper still buzzing in her hand. Just as she was about to ask him what had his attention so focused that he couldn't respond, she noticed he was laid out on his back fast asleep. Nia was comfortable in a kitchen but knew she couldn't cook like Ms. Ali so either he was hungry, tired or both.

Nia never took an interest in searching through Jihad's personal affects, but she thought rather than wake him up, she'd just text whoever was trying to reach him and let the person know he was sleeping. What she saw next jolted her from the inside out. It seemed like an infinite series of the numbers "123" and "143" displayed in the tiny window of Jihad's beeper. Nia had no idea who the young woman was that had taken the time to impress upon Jihad how much she missed (123) and loved (143) him but she had every intention of waking his ass up and finding out. Anybody with a beeper knew there were various numerical abbreviations that meant different things. Obviously, if someone sent you a beep with 911; they needed you to call back ASAP. But in this moment, Nia knew that the sender of these back-to-back texts missed and loved Jihad. The question was WHY, and Nia planned on finding out… now! The beeper also displayed the number of the sender, but Nia decided not to give the girl the satisfaction of asking her questions that this peacefully resting man could answer himself.

"Jihad!", Nia screamed, snatching the covers back off of him. He changed positions but didn't awaken. Nia's anger was quickly rising, and she was doing everything in her power to restrain herself. It didn't take long for emotions of fury to overtake her as she threw his beeper at his torso. Jihad jumped up, scrambling to make sense of what was going on.

"Damn, Nia what's up?" Nia could barely wait for him to get the words out of his mouth before she began to rattle off questions that she hoped he would answer intelligibly for all of their sake.

"Who is beeping you from 305-201-1240"? "And what reason have you given her to luvvvvv and misssss you so badly? This chick has been blowing this pager up for the past 20 minutes and I want to know what's up?"

The puzzled look on Jihad's face only infuriated Nia more and she was just about to explode with a series of additional questions when he stepped back as if he thought it best to put a little more distance between them.

"Nia, I don't know what you're talking about, but I want you to calm down before this goes left really quick." Jihad's tone was calm, but Nia saw the intensity and rising anger in his eyes and realized that she wasn't the only one that could turn up.

"Jihad, you want me to calm down when clearly something has been going on behind my back?" Nia asked this rhetorical question, already knowing that was exactly what Jihad expected of her. Nevertheless, she too was growing angrier and wanted some answers immediately.

Jihad sat on the edge of the bed, irritated that he had been awakened from his sleep. He pressed the buttons on his pager so that he could view the multiple messages from this unrecognizable number. He knew that Nia wouldn't want to hear this, but he really didn't know the number or the sender. "Nia, I don't know who sent these messages. How do you know the person doesn't have the wrong number? I shouldn't have to prove anything but if you're gonna keep tripping, we can straighten this with a phone call." It was something about the way Jihad spoke the last sentence that made Nia feel immature. Even though any reasonable person could see how she arrived at the conclusions that she did. Nia knew Jihad but more importantly, she trusted him. So, she chose to let it go … at least for now.

Jihad was glad Nia had let it go but he hadn't. He recognized the phone number and was pretty sure it belonged to one of his twin sister's friends. The question was why would one of the twins' friends be sending these beeper messages to his phone? Jihad knew that his family missed him and had preferred if he had chosen to attend a local college or university if he insisted on pursuing this school thing. He hated to think that someone would try to sabotage his relationship just to get him back in Miami, but this didn't make sense. He wasn't losing any sleep over it, but it was on his radar and eventually he planned to get to the bottom of it.

He couldn't even be mad at Nia 'cause if the shoe were on the other foot, he couldn't promise that he'd maintain his composure either.

Chapter Thirty-Two

The Set, more like Rattler Central, was the gathering spot on FAMU's campus, was covered with orange and green-draped graduate candidates anticipating this momentous day. Today preparation and opportunity would meet and afford many FAMU Alumni positions in their respected fields of study with topnotch corporations and institutions. Many had gathered in tradition to take pictures with friends and family before heading to the Tallahassee Civic Center for the official graduation ceremony. Nia was overwhelmed with gratitude for her parents, professors, and Jihad for having her back with encouragement and support throughout the years. Today was the day. There were unexpected hiccups along the way like having to take Psychological Statistics three times just to be eligible for graduation but at this point, Nia reflected with pride because she had not allowed her weaknesses to diminish her determination. Nia had even learned to laugh at the experience that had at one point brought her to tears.

Nia, Jihad, Mr. and Ms. Ali, and Jaz were standing together as (one of the twin's) snapped their picture. Nia was so happy that Jihad's sisters and their boyfriends had joined them for the occasion. She hadn't seen them in a while but enjoyed chatting with them on the phone from time to time. The twins enjoyed the VIP treatment in the streets of Miami. Their family's name carried weight and they pretty much got their way in their hood.

The twins looked beautiful, dressed in matching floral two-piece white pant sets. The bright orange, yellow, pink, and green flowers complimented their caramel colored skin tones. One twin was just a little taller than the other but other than that you couldn't tell them apart. Jihad was so overprotective of them and kept his eyes on their boyfriends as their hands continuously wrapped around the girls' waists and then comfortably rested on their derrieres. Jihad knew the twins were young adults now and that they were in Miami feeling themselves, but they would always be his little sisters and he had to remind himself to play it cool, so he didn't ruin this day for Nia and her family.

The Civic Center was the largest arena style venue in Tallahassee, and it was quickly filling up with friends, family, professors, deans and dignitaries who were here to celebrate the Florida Agricultural and Mechanical University's Class of 1994 as they take their final step of this collegiate journey. Today, they would receive degrees in any area of study imaginable because of the parents, professors, school leadership, and most importantly their commitment to stay the course of excellence on the highest of seven hills, at their beloved FAMU.

Everyone settled in their seats and the arena's lights flashed a few times, signaling that the commencement

THORNS OF ROSES

program was about to begin. A gentleman's baritone voice could be heard over the PA asking everyone to please stand to their feet as FAMU's elite chorus leads us in the National Anthem. FAMU President, stood tall in stature and was well known for his commitment to Rattler excellence, spirit, and pride, rose to cheers of whoops and hollers from the graduating class and alumni alike.

"Good afternoon, to the graduating class of 1994. We do not take lightly the hard work, dedication, and persistence that earned your right to be here today. Nor do we minimize the significant influence of your various support systems that have helped you by way of finances, encouraging guidance, tough love, and all the necessary components that move an individual from college freshman to college graduate. Regardless of your chosen field of study, you are now prepared to take the nurturing, knowledge, and extraordinary experiences of being a Rattler into a world that awaits your innovation, gifts, talents, and willingness to contribute to its progression. I invite the graduating class to look around and behold the greatness that surrounds you and thrives within you. Go forth with wisdom, courage, and faith; because you have stayed the course, you are our ancestors' wildest dreams come true. There is no corner of earth that you cannot influence and even if you grow weary from time to time, rest but never quit."

Families and friends of the graduates whooped and hollered as the name of their loved one was called upon. Loud cheers bounced off the walls of the standing room only arena.

One by one young men and women draped in green or orange caps and gowns crossed the stage, shook hands of school and county officials and received the single most important document that certified they had reached another milestone in their lives, college graduate. Nia felt like she was walking on air. She couldn't put how she felt into words; it was just a great feeling of accomplishment, pride, and belief that she would live the life she'd dreamt of since childhood.

As parents and other attendees exited the arena to greet the Class of 1994, they were directed to large tents that had been labeled with the initials of the graduates' last names. Jaz was the first to see the white tent labeled with large black letters, P-S, and pointed for the group to see where Nia would meet them outside. It didn't take long for Nia to recognize her family and friends and she quickly walked up to them and gave her parents a hug. The others were eager to congratulate Nia as she hugged each person one by one. Nia had caught a glimpse of Jihad from the corner of her eye and her heart did a little dance as she approached him. Never big on words, Jihad's lips slightly parted as he gave Nia "their look". As the two embraced, both Nia and Jihad connected on so many levels. They had shared many conversations about life and their dreams and today was a win for not only Nia, but Jihad as well. He was so proud that she had stayed focused and accomplished her goal. College towns are notorious for the party scenes including drinking and drug use, yet Nia and her classmates had not succumb to the trappings that could detour or destroy one's dreams.

Nia had missed the conversation between Jihad and his twin sisters but when they got a few moments alone, he clued her in on his decision to discontinue his studies at TCC and move back home. At first, she was disappointed because she could see that Jihad had really begun to look forward to his classes. Every now and then, he'd share something that was discussed in one of them and she could tell that he was intrigued and enjoyed most of what he was learning at school. He'd maintained an excellent GPA so internally Nia struggled with him going back to Miami before earning his degree. Jihad didn't explain the details of the conversation between him and his sisters, but his body language and tone let Nia know that he had made his mind up and that meant they were moving back to Miami. She didn't press the issue; family dynamics could be sensitive, so she trusted that Jihad was doing what he thought was best. He had always had her back and there was no doubt that wherever their paths led she had his.

Chapter Thirty-Three

Nia had planned on applying for a teaching position in Tallahassee upon graduation but when Jihad decided to return to Miami, she applied for teaching positions in the Miami-Dade County Public School system. There were very few available positions in the spring and recruiters had advised to her to continuously check the job listings between May and August. By July, teachers who were retiring, resigning, or transferring to other schools, would have submitted their intentions to the Human Resources Department and more jobs would become available before the start of the new school year in August. One of Nia's friends mentioned that the City of Miami Police Department was hiring Communications Assistants and Communications Operators to answer 911 calls and dispatch the police. When Nia mentioned it to Jihad, he didn't seem to have an opinion one way or the other, but Nia thought it would be an exciting opportunity and she already knew a few people working for the department that she could use as references on her application. The hiring process was pretty straight forward; submit the application, take a typing test, pass a drug and background check, take a polygraph test, and complete the panel interview. It sounded like a lot, but Nia successfully completed the process and was offered a job as a Communications Operator.

All the crime shows Nia had enjoyed watching over the years could not prepare her for the vast and intricate world of law enforcement. Communications was the hub and nucleus that connected the citizens and uniformed officers. The 911 call takers and dispatchers were responsible for ensuring that emergency and non- emergency situations were handled with excellent communication skills, efficient information gathering, and thorough transmission of the level of danger citizens and officers oftentimes found themselves in from day to day.

Dee was a no-nonsense veteran dispatcher and trainer assigned to train Nia for the duration of the year-long program. As Nia sat in the seat next to Dee at the console, Dee wasted no time reiterating the level of precision, proficiency, and accuracy required to successfully complete the training course.

"When you sit at this console, you are the direct link between our citizens and our uniformed officers. Every officer patrolling the streets wants and deserves to go home to his or her family. Your job is to work as the eyes and ears of the officers until they arrive on the scene of a call and continue to provide pertinent information provided by people who call in to report a crime so that we simultaneously protect our citizens and officers in the safest manner possible." Nia didn't know whether to thank Dee for the insight or get up and bolt out of there. She was excited about the job but the intensity in Dee's voice gave deeper meaning of what the job called for in comparison to the job's description written advertisement. Dee noticed the skepticism in Nia's eyes and reached out to give her hand a gentle squeeze. "You're going to do well, let's get started."

Nia learned so much about the fast paced, life-saving audible transmissions that Dee and the other dispatchers conducted over the air, some days for up to 16 hours a day. The 911 call takers were the first line of support for citizens calling in about being in immediate danger themselves, witnessing crimes taking place in real time, or calling to be transferred to the fire and rescue department for emergency medical assistance. The word intense didn't accurately describe the day-to-day operations of the Communications department. Dispatchers were receiving detailed, life-depending information from the call takers while simultaneously translating the information to officers enroute to in-progress situations. Blaring police sirens, escalated adrenaline and multiple tiered communication dialogue between call takers, dispatchers, police officers, and shift supervisors, all trying to ascertain the most accurate information from various citizens all at the same time was, for lack of a better word, intense. Dee was an amazing dispatcher and she had impeccable multi-tasking skills. Even when she was dispatching to horrific crime scenes, she was in her own zone, maintaining professionalism, proactiveness, and commitment to help the officers arrive on the scene as informed as possible. By the fourth month of training, Nia had felt nearly every emotion from fear, exhilaration, hope,

THORNS OF ROSES

helplessness to anger and more. The day-to day emotional roller coaster of dispatching had helped her to decide to transition to a call taker position. Answering 911 calls was not for the faint at heart but it did take the direct communication with the officers out of the equation. Call takers still had to multitask with attention to detail, but it better suited Nia and she was assigned to another no-nonsense trainer, Renee. Several months later, Nia and the other communication assistant trainees had learned every major thoroughfare within the city of Miami, how to run background checks for officers, communicate citizens' observations to the dispatchers, and more. One of the most difficult calls Nia answered was a young lady whose brother had apparently gone wild and began shooting members of their family as she fled the scene in fear.

"City of Miami Police, this is Operator 7, what is the nature of your emergency?" Before the caller could answer, Nia heard loud boom sounds, 'boom", "boom, boom, boom".

"Hello, Nia said with urgency."

"Help! Help! My brother is trying to kill us. He already shot my parents." Nia immediately begins to ascertain the information; all while her heartbeat is quickly accelerating. Nia rattles off a series of questions while typing the information into the system for dispatch and notifying fire rescue of an in-progress shooting with victims on the scene.

"What is your name? Verify your address and the number you are calling from? "What complexion is your brother? What is his (approximate) height and weight? What color clothing is he wearing? What color are his shoes? Where is he now? Do you know what kind of weapon he is using? Are there other weapons at the location?"

The caller interrupts Nia with screams, "Ma'am please hurry up!" "Come now! He shot my parents and I'm hiding!" Nia continues calmly but is clearly aware of the fright in the caller's voice. "I have officers enroute. Please continue to answer my questions so that we can get the officers and fire rescue to you as quickly as possible." The caller's voice cracked as she did her best to answer Nia's questions. Nia could hear and feel the fear and desperation in her voice and silently prayed that the shooter would be apprehended quickly.

"I am going to stay on the line with you; we have officers enroute.

Where are you now?"

"I'm in a back room but I'm about to crawl out of the window. I don't hear anything now. I don't know where my brother is, and I don't hear anything from my parents."

"Before you crawl out the window, please give me a description of what you have on and let me find out how soon the officers will be there." Nia called the dispatcher handling the call and was informed that the officers were arriving on the scene. Nia unmuted the caller's line and advised her to stay hidden where she was until the officers entered and made contact with her.

Crime scenes take hours; even days to process but later in the week Nia followed up and was told the young lady's parents didn't make it, her brother was arrested, and she would now have to live her life traumatized by the calamity of what she had witnessed and escaped.

Chapter Thirty-Four

Nia worked for the police department for three years before deciding that she really wanted to pursue a career in education. She had learned so much during her tenure as a communications assistant, but her passion was working with children. As a young girl, she had role played with her younger sister, Jaz, and Nia was always the teacher. Sometimes Jaz would resist having to always play the student, but Nia insisted that because she was the oldest, naturally, she should be the teacher. Once again, Nia submitted an application for employment to the human resources department of MDCPS but this time she was called within a few days for an interview at a middle school. Mr. Parker, the principal liked Nia's enthusiasm and after asking her several standard interview questions, he took his glasses off, leaned back in his high back, chocolate brown leather chair and asked Nia,

"What is the difference between you and the other five candidates that are interviewing for this position?"

Nia didn't have a lot of interviewing experience, but she had been 'Nia Ali' since birth. She sat up straight and looked Mr. Parker directly in his eyes and replied, "I don't know the other four candidates, but I do know that I was born to teach. I am not applying to teach a subject;

I am asking for an opportunity to help positively impact the lives of the students in communities much like the one I grew up in. I don't have formal teaching experience, but I know the content, I love helping others, and I'm a team player. More importantly, if I ever perceive that my efforts are not moving children forward, you will never have to ask me to leave; I will remove myself."

Mr. Parker's poker face didn't give Nia a hint of his acceptance or rejection of her response. He told her that after all the interviews were complete, his secretary would notify her if she had gotten the job or not. He stood up first and then walked Nia out to the school foyer. Shaking her hand, he said it had been a pleasure meeting Ms. Nia Ali. Nia couldn't be certain, but she felt confident that she had gotten the job.

Jihad and Nia had found a condo with ocean views in the Hallandale Beach area and had finally settled back into life close to their home city. Jihad was managing family business and acquiring real estate for land development projects and Nia was now in her second year of teaching a writing and humanities course to middle school students. Mr. Parker's secretary, Mrs. Carter, had called Nia the same evening of her interview and officially offered her the job. Nia must've jumped three feet off the ground with excitement at the news and was even selected as the Rookie Teacher of the Year to represent her school in the annual district selection.

Jihad hadn't mentioned TCC or school since moving back home but Nia often wondered if he missed it. He always encouraged her to pursue her goals and dreams and she just wanted to do the same for him. It was a hard balancing act when you were trying to support someone but also be sensitive to his or her need to handle their situation in the best way, they saw fit. Nia and Jihad had unbreakable bond and they comforted each other in verbal and non-verbal ways. He knew she was a borderline nerd, as one of her cousins had always referred to her and he would take time from his schedule to visit local book stores searching for books that he thought might interest her. She would cook his favorite foods, mostly vegetarian dishes, and be sure to wear body fragrance, soft, lace nighties and help him to relax with occasional body massages.

Life was good. Nia enjoyed being able to hang out with her girls and Miami never disappointed on nightlife or adventure. There was always a club, concert, new eatery, car show, play tours, comedy shows or retail therapy to take your mind off the everyday challenges of life. The best part of being home was being close to Momma. She had been the cornerstone of Nia's life; always willing to slice a piece of pie, pull up a chair and just chat about any and everything. Nia was forever grateful for her experiences at FAMU but for her, there really was no place like home.

Jihad had stopped by one of the couple's favorite Caribbean restaurants and picked up dinner on his way home. He was very particular about his diet and didn't care for red meat. However, he considered himself more of a pescatarian and ordered himself a stewed fish entrée. Fond of spicy foods, Nia was happy to see that he'd ordered her the jerk chicken, rice and peas, and cabbage meal.

Jihad flipped through the sports channels trying to find a game worth watching as Nia ate and contemplated what the couple could get into over the weekend. No sooner than she had finished her dinner, she got a sickening feeling in her stomach and felt a sudden need to rush to the bathroom. Startled by her actions, Jihad, rushed behind her to make sure she was okay. As he approached the glass entry door, saw Nia on her knees with her head over the commode. She could not stop the regurgitation of the meal she had moments ago thoroughly enjoyed. Jihad sprung into action and retrieved some towels from the linen closet, running hot water over one before giving it to Nia to wipe the beads of sweat from her head and her mouth.

Nia had been so consumed with work, hanging out with her friends and family, and living the life she and Jihad were building, she hadn't noticed that she had missed two months of her menstrual cycle. After the vomiting episode, her mind quickly reverted to the missed periods, and she asked Jihad to go to the pharmacy to get a pregnancy test. Jihad would do just about anything for Nia but running out for feminine products had to be the least likeable thing that he wanted to do. Nevertheless, just the thought of Nia being pregnant filled him with excitement and joy, he didn't hesitate to get his keys and go get the test.

Nia was so nervous, she asked Jihad to read the instructions while she went into the bathroom to 'take' the test. This was probably the only test in Nia's life she felt she couldn't fail. Regardless of the outcome, she was sharing her life with her first love, working in the career of her passion, and now possibly embarking on becoming a mommy. For a quick second she thought about her mother who would surely encourage her to marry Jihad if they loved each other and planned on having a family but honestly neither Nia nor Jihad had seen many successful marriages in their childhood, so she focused more on the love between them and not ceremonious titles to define their relationship.

Nia carefully followed the instructions that Jihad read aloud to her and when finished she washed her hands and used a paper towel to pass the test to Jihad. She didn't know what single or double lines on the small window of the test meant but when she handed it to Jihad, his big goofy grin let her know they were about to be parents. Nia's grin must have looked just as goofy to Jihad because they burst out laughing as he hugged her and lifted her off the ground.

Jihad began jokingly teasing Nia saying, "You see what happens when you can't keep your hands off me". Nia laughed at Jihad, rolling her eyes as if to say, "Boy, please". They showered together, both quiet; both thinking their private thoughts about how life was about to change in the most beautiful way.

Chapter Thirty-Five

Nia's pregnancy was enough to make her vow to never have more children. She was sick the entire nine months. She had been diagnosed with Extreme Hyperemesis , severe morning sickness. She couldn't work because she was bed ridden and received weekly visits from a nurse to change her IV and check her iron levels. She couldn't imagine how women went through it but her mother told her not everyone experiences pregnancy in the same ways. It was Ms. Ali and Jihad that kept Nia sane during her pregnancy. She could only eat a select diet and even healthy foods made her vomit. Jihad was so kind and loving, which helped Nia not focus on being confined to their home and mostly to the bed. Since she couldn't leave home for extended periods of time, he would bring catalogues of baby's furniture and clothing home and spend time with her picking out paint colors for the nursery to help take her mind off her condition.

The months continued to pass and before they knew it, Nia was counting down the days til her due date. She was awakened one night by a horrible dream that something was wrong with her baby. She woke Jihad up from his sleep and insisted that they go to the emergency room immediately. Jihad had heard that women turned into totally different people during pregnancy, and he was reluctant to rush Nia to the ER based on a dream. He knew that once Nia's mind was set on something, he would get no rest until they went to check on the baby. He put on a gray joggers and a white t-shirt and helped Nia get dressed in a button down shirtdress. He disconnected the IV from her arm and put her slippers on her feet as she sat on the accent chair near the bed. He called the valet downstairs and asked that someone bring his truck to the front due to a medical emergency. A front lobby attendant brought a wheelchair up to their residence and assisted Jihad in getting Nia downstairs and into the car.

    Jihad could tell by Nia's silence that her dream had really disturbed her, and he silently prayed that it was just a dream. As he walked Nia into the hospital ER, a nurse helped get her into a wheel chair and registered to be examined. The visit began with standard operating procedures; provide personal information, insurance card, emergency contact information, and wait to be called back by a nurse. Nia nor Jihad was prepared for what happened next. After the nurse checked her blood pressure and assigned her a room to be examined, a doctor entered and explained that the baby's heart rate was barely detectable. He spoke clearly but quickly and informed the couple that Nia would have to have her labor induced and the labor and delivery department staff would be in shortly to prepare her for labor. Nia and Jihad exchanged looks of fright and both silently prayed that their baby would be okay. Jihad was being strong for Nia but he was on the edge. Nia had told him that she had dreamt something was wrong and he prayed that they'd made it to the hospital in time. Nia was normally composed and kept a cool head under pressure but right now she was scared. Jihad leaned down and whispered to Nia's belly "Lord please protect our baby and give him or her strength to hold on while the doctors attended to Nia".

Jihad never left Nia's side, but he stepped back from her bedside long enough to call their parents and let them know what was going on. Ms. Ali barely let Jihad finish explaining before she was getting dressed and hanging up the phone to head towards the hospital. Time seemed to stand still even though there were several things happening at once. An anesthesiologist, registered nurse, OB GYN, and other staff were all moving fast to get Nia into the delivery room. Ms. Ali called Jihad's phone and asked to put Nia's ear to the phone. "Nia, you are my daughter, but you are God's daughter first. You and your unborn child's lives rest solely in the Almighty's hands. Do not be afraid and have faith that everything is going to be okay. I'm on my way to meet my grandbaby." Nia handed Jihad the phone and felt a sense of relief as she started following instructions of the midwife that was assisting in her delivery.

Nia believed in the power of prayer. She had witnessed the atmosphere change when her grandmother would pray for and with her family. When that last push birthed baby Laila into the world, Nia held her breath until she heard their princess make her first cry, but she heard nothing. As soon as Laila was born, the nurses whisked her away and within minutes returned her to her mother's bare chest. Laila's umbilical cord had been wrapped around her neck three times, which had restricted her breathing. Once Jihad cut the cord and the nurses took her out of the delivery room, she received a procedure to increase her oxygen and stimulate her breathing. She was so beautiful with a head full with dark curly hair and rosy cheeks as she lay on her mother. Ms. Ali had made it to the delivery room and Jihad had hugged her in relief. He stood near Nia's bedside and silently thanked God that Nia's dream hadn't been a nightmare.

Chapter Thirty-Six

Baby Laila was the pride and joy of her parents and grandparents' lives. There hadn't been a baby in their immediate family in a while, so she was the center of attention, and everyone doted on her. Jihad's mother had volunteered to babysit Laila during her first year, not hearing of sending her to a daycare with so many other children. She got no argument from the couple, and they loved that Laila was in the best of care during their absence.

G-Ma as they affectionately named Queen would give a full account of Laila's day, which included her nap times, if she was fretful, or how much she cooed when being held by her G-Ma. Time moved swiftly and even though both Laila and Queen loved their time together, it was a sacrifice from her business operations, and they all decided Laila would go to daycare after her 1st birthday. Nia was so grateful for all the love and care Queen had shown Laila; she had not been sick once during her days with her G-Ma.

Laila's first birthday was a huge production. Despite Jihad's disapproval, Nia had planned a party to remember for their baby girl's first birthday. Jihad wasn't opposed to a celebration but thought Laila was too young to enjoy or appreciate all the details Nia had planned.

Nia, on the other hand, felt that Laila's first birthday was worthy of an all-out extravaganza, and she spared no expense. When Jihad realized he couldn't talk Nia out of having a big party, he conceded and ensured that all the vendors were paid and ready for his princess' big day. Pony rides, clowns, train rides, several bounce houses, shrimp kabobs, corn on the cobb, barbecue chicken, potato salad, pigeon peas and rice, baked beans, string beans, several cakes, cupcakes, candy apples, cotton candy, and more were all a part of the grand celebration. A professional photographer was on hand to capture all of the family and friends' children having the time of their lives and of course, the birthday girl who pretty much was unaware of all the hoopla going on around her for her. By the time it was time to sing happy birthday and eat cake, Laila was fast asleep in her stroller, sprawled out on her back. Jihad jokingly scolded Nia, telling her that this was her party, not Laila's but he too had enjoyed celebrating their daughter's first birthday with loved ones.

Much like the baby shower they'd had nearly two years before, several family members volunteered to help transport Laila's gifts to the couple's residence. Jihad appreciated the gesture, but he didn't relax the guard of protection he had for his family. He sent one of his homeboys to a local truck rental center and had him to rent a truck large enough to get everything home in one trip. Even in the midst of all the party celebration, Jihad always had a sixth sense about not trusting smiling faces. He'd witnessed the devastation of blind trust and he didn't underestimate anyone. When his homie returned to the park with the truck, they loaded it up with all the gifts and Nia secured Laila in her car seat and followed Jihad home. They decided after a long day, they'd return the truck the following day.

Chapter Thirty-Seven

The condo was perfect for the couple when they returned home from college in Tally but now as Nia scanned the room while standing in the foyer, she could barely see any of the white marble floor due to all the gifts crowding the space. Jihad must have been reading her mind because he exited the floor to ceiling mirrored bathroom doors and stood in the hallway without saying anything for a few minutes. Nia and Jihad both spoke at the same time and burst into laughter as they basically said, "This isn't going to work" at the same time. Nia attempted to organize all the gift-wrapped bags and boxes but there was only so much space. Jihad must have been reading Nia's mind because later as they lay in bed, he mentioned that it was time for them to look for a home; somewhere Laila could have a backyard and more space for their family.

The first couple of months, house hunting was exciting but after a while Nia felt overwhelmed with all the details of choosing a home. Cul de sac, open floor plans, one or two levels, subdivision or not, private baths or Jack and Jill and the options were limitless. They had narrowed their choice of neighborhoods down to two; West Miramar or Pembroke Pines and after the first month, Jihad had pretty much left the task of selecting "the one" to Nia. When Nia pulled up to the future site of a single-family home subdivision in West Miramar, she knew it was where she wanted to live. There were only a few homes currently being built but the landscape was exquisite; tall palm trees, lush green plants with annual multi-color blooms with large cascading waterfalls on each side of the two-lane entryway. The tall, large, round, concrete columns were adorned by decorative black iron gates, which were manned by an armed security guard. Nia thought to herself, "If they have a security guard and the houses aren't even built yet, this place is going to really be something when it's finished." She pulled up to the covered security office and a gentleman stepped out to ask her a few questions. Nia felt like she was on an interview. She had to provide her driver's license, pull-up so the security officer could copy her tag, put a color-coded entry pass on her dashboard, and wait for the security guard to announce her entry to the realtor awaiting visitors in the model home. If everyone would have to go through this process enter, Nia knew Jihad would approve.

The middle-aged white woman awaiting Nia at the door introduced herself as Melinda, the Director of Sales for Enchanted Estates. Nia noticed she looked a bit taken aback as she reached out to shake Nia's hand. Nia couldn't figure out if it was her age, race or something totally unrelated that caused a slight change in Melinda's demeanor nor did she concern herself with the reason. Nia was confident in her pursuit to find a home and proceeded to express her interest in viewing the various floor plans and elevation options for the coming home sites. Melinda seemed to relax and maintained professional decorum after Nia pulled a prequalification letter from her monogramed LV tote bag and handed it to her. Nia thought to herself, "I wouldn't be here if I couldn't be here so let's find a home for my family."

Jihad looked over the brochures and visual depictions of the homes that would be built within the Enchanted Estates Subdivision. The starting price of the homes was 500k, which didn't seem to bother Jihad. Nia had been able to save the majority of her teaching salary over the last few years because Jihad had paid their condo's monthly rent. The owner had offered to sell it to them, but they had explained that their family was outgrowing the place despite their love of being so close to the ocean. Nia had loved sitting on the panoramic balcony and watching the sunrise or enjoying the sounds of the waves crashing against the shore.

They had packed their personal effects and were ready for the movers to wrap the furniture and wall pictures in protective packaging. It had taken a little more time than promised for their new home to be built but with the unpredictable weather, delays were inevitable. As Nia, continued to monitor that the move was going smoothly and Jihad was on the balcony, holding Laila, as he gazed upon the ocean. Private yachts passed and he could see the swift movement of jet skis bypassing each other along the waterway. Jihad had kept a smile on his face for the sake of not alarming Nia but he was overwhelmed. Holding his daughter calmed his mind; gave him reason to pause and reflect. The college thing was worth a try, but he didn't really have time to go back now that he was working for the family business again. He was happy to help, and he was compensated well. It just seemed at times, he stilled yearned to pursue something of his own.

"Jihad", Nia called out, breaking his stream of thoughts. "What's up?" He replied.

"The movers are just about ready to finish up. I have Laila's car seat in my car already, so we can follow the movers to the house. Are you going to follow us over there?"

Jihad thought about it but realized the move would take at least a few hours. He decided to meet them at the new house after running an errand that he couldn't delay til later. "Nah, ya'll go ahead, I have a stop to make. I'll be there in an hour or two."

"Okay, sounds good," Nia replied.

The movers had unloaded and unpacked the furniture and set it up according to Nia's instructions. She had already scheduled to meet with an interior decorator for some help with filling the large home. The décor from the condo would work for a short while but Nia was looking forward to creating a beautiful space for her family in their gorgeous split level home. Jihad paid the balance on the moving bill before heading out to do his thing, so Nia gave the guys a tip for being so thorough. Several hours had passed and it wasn't like Jihad to not have called or checked on them. She had fed Laila and she was resting in her nursery with the baby monitors nearby. Nia continued to organize Laila's room, but her mind was distracted with thoughts of Jihad.

After cleaning up and unpacking many of the boxes, Nia dialed Jihad's phone. After several attempts, he still had not answered. By now Nia couldn't focus on anything except Jihad and didn't know if she should be upset or worried that he wasn't answering. Worry overtook her and she began to call around to the few people that may have known his whereabouts. A few didn't answer and for the ones who did, they hadn't seen him. Nia's heartbeat was accelerating, and her thoughts were all over the place. She knew something wasn't right. Jihad would never allow her to call this many times back to back without answering. Even if he were busy, he would have had someone to let her know that he'd return her call shortly. Nia's stomach had jitters and it took everything in her not to snatch Laila out of the crib and go look for him. The only problem was she didn't have a clue where to start. She left messages on the twins' phones; not wanting to alarm them, she only said, "Hey give me a call when you get this."

Chapter Thirty-Eight

Mentally in and out of awareness, Nia only heard half of the pastor's and funeral director's final comments. Somewhere between *"To be absent from the body is to be present with the Lord"* and *"Please return to your vehicles, turn your headlights off, and proceed to the repast address on the back of the obituary"*, she was numb from the crown of her head to the soles of her feet.

Nia's heart began to palpitate as her mind raced with a myriad of thoughts and questions.

'How can I leave the man I've known since we were teenagers in this lifeless, barren ground? Jihad was the only man with whom I'd entrusted my heart and virginity, laughed, cried, and grown up with. Together, we brought life into the world and created a beautiful life of dreams." Nia couldn't fathom how Jihad was now *'absent from his body and present with the Lord'.* "The word absent didn't begin to express the emptiness I felt. Jihad was full of life with big dreams and impeccable work ethic. His loyalty was praised by all who knew him and yet today none of that mattered. Somehow tragedy had struck our lives and now I was burying my friend,*

lover and soulmate along with parts of the woman I had grown to be.

How could I gather the strength and presence of mind to return home to our baby girl who cried uncontrollably during the weekend-long search that led to the discovery of her father's lifeless body? The agonizing reality of his ballooned remains floating along a Miami river, behind the homes of a residential subdivision had taken one life and collapsed a family. Heavy hearted and broken spirited, what was I going to do and whom was I going to become in the absence of the other half of me?

Despite the personal strengths and attributes that had always served me well in my relationship, career, and friendships, I now felt lost, alone, numb and weak in a new reality that I couldn't have seen coming and without a doubt would change our lives forever.

How does one stand in complete happiness, planning a beautiful future for your family with the one you love one day and within a blinking of the human eye, find yourself burying your love, dreams, and strength in a solemn, lonely cemetery one week later?"

The tears would not stop falling as Nia pulled up to their home with their beautiful daughter in the back seat. She couldn't help but think, *"This has to be a terrible nightmare."* She could barely muster up the strength to open her car door, slowly making her way around to the rear passenger side to remove Laila from her car seat. Her daughter didn't make a sound as she lay her head on her mother's shoulder. Nia knew that at two years old, Laila could not process this great void but Nia could sense that she did. Nia had rejected her family's suggestions of she and the baby staying at her mother's house or having someone to accompany to their home for a few days. Her heart was shattered into millions of pieces, and she just needed to hold her daughter in the bed that she and Jihad had slept in just weeks before, planning a life they would never have the opportunity to live out together.

Made in the USA
Columbia, SC
29 June 2023